PRAISE FOR TH

"New editions of a host of under-discussed classics of the genre."
—*Reactor Magazine*

"Neglected classics of early 20th-century sci-fi in spiffily designed paperback editions."
—*Financial Times*

"An entertaining, engrossing glimpse into the profound and innovative literature of the early twentieth century."
—*Foreword*

"Shows that 'proto-sf' was being published much more widely, alongside other kinds of fiction, before it emerged as a genre."
—*BSFA Review*

"An excellent start at showcasing the strange wonders offered by the Radium Age."
—*Shelf Awareness*

"Lovingly curated . . . The series' freedom from genre purism lets us see how a specific set of anxieties—channeled through dystopias, Lovecraftian horror, arch social satire, and adventure tales—spurred literary experimentation and the bending of conventions."
—*Los Angeles Review of Books*

"A huge effort to help define a new era of science fiction."
—*Transfer Orbit*

"Admirable . . . and highly recommended."
—*Washington Post*

"Long live the Radium Age."
—*Los Angeles Times*

BEFORE SUPERMAN

The Radium Age Book Series
Joshua Glenn

Voices from the Radium Age, edited by Joshua Glenn, 2022

A World of Women, J. D. Beresford, 2022

The World Set Free, H. G. Wells, 2022

The Clockwork Man, E. V. Odle, 2022

Nordenholt's Million, J. J. Connington, 2022

Of One Blood, Pauline Hopkins, 2022

What Not, Rose Macaulay, 2022

The Lost World and The Poison Belt, Arthur Conan Doyle, 2023

Theodore Savage, Cicely Hamilton, 2023

The Napoleon of Notting Hill, G. K. Chesterton, 2023

The Night Land, William Hope Hodgson, 2023

More Voices from the Radium Age, edited by Joshua Glenn, 2023

Man's World, Charlotte Haldane, 2024

The Inhumans and Other Stories: A Selection of Bengali Science Fiction, edited and translated by Bodhisattva Chattopadhyay, 2024

The People of the Ruins, Edward Shanks, 2024

The Heads of Cerberus and Other Stories, Francis Stevens, edited by Lisa Yaszek, 2024

The Greatest Adventure, John Taine, 2025

The Hampdenshire Wonder, J. D. Beresford, 2025

Before Superman: Superhumans of the Radium Age, edited by Joshua Glenn, 2025

Yankees in Petrograd, Marietta S. Shaginyan, translated and introduced by Jill Roese, 2025

BEFORE SUPERMAN

SUPERHUMANS OF THE RADIUM AGE

edited and introduced by Joshua Glenn

THE MIT PRESS
CAMBRIDGE, MASSACHUSETTS
LONDON, ENGLAND

The MIT Press
Massachusetts Institute of Technology
77 Massachusetts Avenue, Cambridge, MA 02139
mitpress.mit.edu

© 2025 Massachusetts Institute of Technology

All rights reserved. No part of this book may be used to train artificial intelligence systems or reproduced in any form by any electronic or mechanical means (including photocopying, recording, or information storage and retrieval) without permission in writing from the publisher.

The MIT Press would like to thank the anonymous peer reviewers who provided comments on drafts of this book. The generous work of academic experts is essential for establishing the authority and quality of our publications. We acknowledge with gratitude the contributions of these otherwise uncredited readers.

This book was set in Arnhem Pro and PF DIN Text Pro by New Best-set Typesetters Ltd. Printed and bound in the United States of America.

Library of Congress Cataloging-in-Publication Data

Names: Glenn, Joshua, 1967– editor, writer of introduction.
Title: Before Superman : superhumans of the radium age / edited and
   introduced by Joshua Glenn.
Description: Cambridge, Massachusetts : The MIT Press, 2025. |
   Series: Radium age
Identifiers: LCCN 2024047179 (print) | LCCN 2024047180 (ebook) |
   ISBN 9780262553070 (paperback) | ISBN 9780262384025 (pdf) |
   ISBN 9780262384032 (epub)
Subjects: LCSH: Science fiction—20th century. | LCGFT: Short stories.
Classification: LCC PN6071.S33 B44 2025 (print) | LCC PN6071.S33 (ebook) |
   DDC 808.83/8762—dc23/eng/20250117
LC record available at https://lccn.loc.gov/2024047179
LC ebook record available at https://lccn.loc.gov/2024047180

10 9 8 7 6 5 4 3 2 1

EU Authorised Representative: Easy Access System Europe, Mustamäe tee 50, 10621 Tallinn, Estonia | Email: gpsr.requests@easproject.com publication supported by

Figure Foundation

CONTENTS

Series Foreword xi
Introduction: *Homo Superior Ex Machina* xvii
Joshua Glenn

1 André Marcueil (1902) 1
   Alfred Jarry

2 Thomas Dunbar (1904) 11
   Francis Stevens

3 Hannibal Lepsius (1909) 29
   M. P. Shiel

4 Léo Saint-Clair (1911) 47
   Jean de La Hire

5 Ralph 124C 41+ (1911–1912) 57
   Hugo Gernsback

6 Young Diana (1917–1918) 73
   Marie Corelli

7 Yva (1919) 81
   H. Rider Haggard

8 Zoo (1921) 93
   George Bernard Shaw

9 Rudy Marek (1922) 113
   Karel Čapek

10 Zuanthrol (1924) 141
   Edgar Rice Burroughs

11 **Rotwang (1925)** 151
    Thea von Harbou

12 **Professor Challenger (1928)** 169
    Arthur Conan Doyle

    List of Contributors 209

SERIES FOREWORD

Joshua Glenn

Do we really know science fiction? There were the scientific romance years that stretched from the mid-nineteenth century to circa 1900. And there was the genre's so-called golden age, from circa 1935 through the early 1960s. But between those periods, and overshadowed by them, was an era that has bequeathed us such tropes as the robot (berserk or benevolent), the tyrannical superman, the dystopia, the unfathomable extraterrestrial, the sinister telepath, and the eco-catastrophe. In 2009, writing for the sf blog io9.com at the invitation of Annalee Newitz and Charlie Jane Anders, I became fascinated with the period during which the sf genre as we know it emerged. Inspired by the exactly contemporaneous career of Marie Curie, who shared a Nobel Prize for her discovery of radium in 1903, only to die of radiation-induced leukemia in 1934, I eventually dubbed this three-decade interregnum the "Radium Age."

Curie's development of the theory of radioactivity, which led to the extraordinary, terrifying, awe-inspiring insight that the atom is, at least in part, a state of energy constantly in movement, is an apt metaphor for the twentieth century's first three decades. These years were marked by rising sociocultural strife across various fronts: the founding of the women's suffrage movement, the National Association for the Advancement of Colored People, socialist currents within the labor movement, anticolonial and revolutionary upheaval around the world . . . as well as the associated strengthening of reactionary movements that supported, for example, racial segregation, immigration restriction, eugenics, and sexist policies.

Science—as a system of knowledge, a mode of experimenting, and a method of reasoning—accelerated the pace of change during these years in ways simultaneously liberating and terrifying. As sf author and historian Brian Stableford points out in his 1989 essay "The Plausibility of the Impossible," the universe we discovered by means of the scientific method in the early twentieth century defies common sense: "We are haunted by a sense of the impossibility of ultimately making sense of things." By playing host to certain far-out notions—time travel, faster-than-light travel, and ESP, for example—that we have every reason to judge impossible, science fiction serves as an "instrument of negotiation," Stableford suggests, with which we strive to accomplish "the difficult diplomacy of existence in a scientifically knowable but essentially unimaginable world." This is no less true today than during the Radium Age.

The social, cultural, political, and technological upheavals of the 1900–1935 period are reflected in the proto-sf writings of authors such as Olaf Stapledon, William Hope Hodgson, Muriel Jaeger, Karel Čapek, G. K. Chesterton, Cicely Hamilton, W. E. B. Du Bois, Yevgeny Zamyatin, E. V. Odle, Arthur Conan Doyle, Mikhail Bulgakov, Pauline

Hopkins, Stanisław Ignacy Witkiewicz, Aldous Huxley, Gustave Le Rouge, A. Merritt, Rudyard Kipling, Rose Macaulay, J. D. Beresford, J. J. Connington, S. Fowler Wright, Jack London, Thea von Harbou, and Edgar Rice Burroughs, not to mention the late-period but still incredibly prolific H. G. Wells himself. More cynical than its Victorian precursor yet less hard-boiled than the sf that followed, in the writings of these visionaries we find acerbic social commentary, shock tactics, and also a sense of frustrated idealism—and reactionary cynicism, too—regarding humankind's trajectory.

The MIT Press's Radium Age series represents a much-needed evolution of my own efforts to champion the best proto-sf novels and stories from 1900 to 1935 among scholars already engaged in the fields of utopian and speculative fiction studies, as well as general readers interested in science, technology, history, and thrills and chills. By reissuing literary productions from a time period that hasn't received sufficient attention for its contribution to the emergence of science fiction as a recognizable form—one that exists and has meaning in relation to its own traditions and innovations, as well as within a broader ecosystem of literary genres, each of which, as John Rieder notes in *Science Fiction and the Mass Cultural Genre System* (2017), is itself a product of overlapping "communities of practice"—we hope not only to draw attention to key overlooked works but perhaps also to influence the way scholars and sf fans alike think about this crucial yet neglected and misunderstood moment in the emergence of the sf genre.

John W. Campbell and other Cold War–era sf editors and propagandists dubbed a select group of writers and story types from the pulp era to be the golden age of science fiction. In doing so, they helped fix in the popular imagination a too-narrow understanding of what the sf genre can offer. (In his introduction to the 1974 collection *Before the Golden Age*, for example, Isaac Asimov notes that although it may have possessed a certain exuberance, in general sf from before the mid-1930s moment when Campbell assumed editorship of *Astounding Stories* "seems, to anyone who has experienced the Campbell Revolution, to be clumsy, primitive, naive.") By returning to an international tradition of scientific speculation via fiction from after the Poe–Verne–Wells era and before sf's Golden Age, the Radium Age series will demonstrate—contra Asimov et al.—the breadth, richness, and diversity of the literary works that were responding to a vertiginous historical period, and how they helped innovate a nascent genre (which wouldn't be named until the mid-1920s, by Hugo Gernsback, founder of *Amazing Stories* and namesake of the Hugo Awards) as a mode of speculative imagining.

The MIT Press's Noah J. Springer and I are grateful to the sf writers and scholars who have agreed to serve as this series' advisory board. Aided by their guidance, we'll endeavor to surface a rich variety of texts, along with introductions by a diverse group of sf scholars, sf writers, and others that will situate these remarkable, entertaining, forgotten works within their own social, political, and scientific contexts, while drawing out contemporary parallels.

We hope that reading Radium Age writings, published in times as volatile as our own, will serve to remind us that our own era's seemingly natural, eternal, and inevitable social, economic, and cultural forms and norms are—like Madame Curie's atom—forever in flux.

INTRODUCTION: *HOMO SUPERIOR EX MACHINA*
Joshua Glenn

Science-fictional narratives depicting the triumphs and tribulations of a superhuman—a human being, that is to say, who via a (purportedly non-magical) catalyst such as mutation, laboratory experiment, or sheer force of will has evolved into a creature stronger, smarter, more gifted, and in certain cases sexier than we mere mortals have any right to be—first became commonplace during the genre's emergent Radium Age (1900–1935). The proto-sf stories and excerpts in this volume will introduce readers to the weird and wonderful ancestors of today's comic-book and cinematic superheroes.

Many authors of Radium Age superhuman tales derived at least some inspiration from the highly speculative theories of evolutionary biology and philosophy that were much-discussed during the early twentieth century. In the first decade of the twentieth century, research was still being conducted by biologists who agreed with the early 19th-century naturalist Lamarck that characteristics acquired by organisms during their lifetime can be transmitted to their offspring. Neo-Lamarckians extrapolated from this hypothesis the notion that organisms may continuously evolve towards a more perfect form because such change is wanted or needed—i.e., by Nature, or Life. (Darwinian theory, by contrast, places organisms entirely at the mercy of their environment.) Some intrepid neo-Lamarckians went so far as to speculate that *homo sapiens* itself might make way—to quote David Bowie, who likely adopted the term from Stan Lee's *X-Men*, though it was first popularized by the proto-sf author Olaf Stapledon—for the *homo superior*.

How to resolve the conflict between neo-Lamarckians and Darwinians? The French philosopher Henri Bergson attempted to do just this via his 1907 treatise *Creative Evolution* . . . which proposes that humankind's evolution is motivated by the *élan vital*—which is to say, by our species' natural creative impulse. Bergson, a public thinker so extraordinarily popular that he'd cause New York's first recorded traffic jam while visiting America to lecture on *Creative Evolution*, was a crucial influence on the Radium Age's superhuman characters. In fact, in J.D. Beresford's 1911 novel *The Hampdenshire Wonder*, a proto-sf novel (recently reissued, with an introduction by Ted Chiang, as an installment in the MIT Press's Radium Age series) that helped pioneer sf speculations about super-intelligence, we discover the narrator perusing Bergson's writings on an English commuter train . . . when he finds his attention wandering to the massive cranium of an infant who turns out to be Victor Stott, the novel's titular wonder.

And what of Nietzsche, you ask? The German philosopher's concept of the *Übermensch*—a goal that humankind ought to set for itself, he urged, in the form of a future generation whose values are creative and life-affirming; and a vision of self-invented "aristocrats" able to overcome in themselves the limitations of their families and culture—can be glimpsed in several Radium Age superhuman stories. Of particular import, perhaps, was the foreboding prediction, made in *Thus Spake Zarathustra*, that even as for "man" (i.e., *homo sapiens*) the mere sight of an ape can serve as a cringe-inducing reminder of our pre-human origins, "just that man shall be for the *Übermensch*: a laughing-stock or a painful embarrassment." Unlike Bergson and neo-Lamarckian science popularizers, Nietzsche imagined his way into a possible future scenario in which a few extraordinary humans have evolved themselves into "over-men." (Nietzsche's *Übermensch* wouldn't be rendered in English as "superman" until 1909, by a translator borrowing terminology from George Bernard Shaw's neo-Lamarckian 1903 play *Man and Superman*.) Mightn't these future prodigies, as Zarathustra claims, be at the very least rather ... scornful towards us non-superhumans?

Nietzsche's *Übermensch* concept would, as we know, by the time of his death in 1900 find itself misappropriated by the worst elements—xenophobes and proto-fascists whom he scorned—in his native country. Thus, in a 1916 essay (by H. Wildon Carr, a Bergsonian philosopher) from the UK theosophical journal *The Quest*, the contributors to which included proto-sf authors such as Algernon Blackwood and Arthur Machen, we read the following passage ... which helps us to comprehend the existential dread (personal and national) underlying some of the superhuman stories from the World War I era.

What is the doctrine which forms for Germany the philosophical justification of this war? It may be summed up in one word,—it is the doctrine of the superman. Germany regards herself as the superman among nations. The doctrine of the superman has been expressed most explicitly by Nietzsche, but for the application of the doctrine, or rather for the adoption of the role by modern Germany, Nietzsche is not responsible.

Robert Grant, an American author, illustrates the Western world's fear of the Teutonic *Übermensch* in "The Superman," a poem reprinted in *A Treasury of War Poetry* (1917): "Ride, Cossacks, ride! Charge, Turcos, charge! The fateful hour has come. / Let all the guns of Britain roar or be forever dumb. / The Superman has burst his bonds. With Kultur-flag unfurled / And prayer on lip he runs amuck, imperilling the world." From World War I on, superhuman-themed fiction would be haunted by the specter of this pseudo-Nietzschean avatar—a tyrant who seeks to ruthlessly subjugate lesser mortals, and who believes themself to be entirely justified in doing so . . . because from their vantage point humankind resembles subhuman vermin. Not that this sort of worldview was exclusively Teutonic, one hastens to note; eugenicists' sterilization initiatives, for example, were well-established in the United States before spreading to Nazi Germany.

Neo-Lamarckian, Bergsonian, and Nietzschean notions of the *homo superior* all trickled into Theosophy—a popular, tirelessly syncretic crypto-religion that influenced or inspired many of the era's anti-conventional creatives, including proto-sf authors from Edgar Rice Burroughs to Robert E. Howard and H.P. Lovecraft. According to

Madame Blavatsky and later Theosophist seers (such as Annie Besant, author of 1900's *The Evolution of Life and Form* and 1913's *Super-Human Men in History & In Religion*), the soul progresses through a series of reincarnations on this and other planets, achieving along the way ever-greater corporeality and higher consciousness. The Theosophical Society offered practical guidance: "Now man, with just a touch of the underdeveloped superman," we read in a 1909 manual published by the American section of the Theosophical Society, "you will know God in his true likeness only when you are more than man—superman." Getting more technical about it, "The Superman in Real Life," an essay published in a 1921 issue of Besant's magazine *The Theosophist*, proclaims that the superman is an adept who has "passed the Fifth Initiation and transcended all human claims and limitations," thus unlocking their new role as a liberator of mankind.

With the above-described influences in mind, most accounts of the emergence of the superhuman as a stock science-fiction character remain content to point out the following dialectic. The proto-sf superhuman is an awe-inspiring figure of fascination, and perhaps even—for those proto-sf authors scornful of aspects of their society and culture—a figure of aspiration, or at the very least identification. Simultaneously, however, the superhuman is a bogeyman who in a best-case scenario will evolve into a benevolent dictator who'll regard us as laughable yet loveable, but who may turn out to be a fuehrer who'll seek to extirpate us from the gene pool! However, we should also consider another dimension of Radium Age proto-sf's fascination with the superhuman—one that's inextricably linked to the early twentieth century's preoccupation with, and dread regarding, the era's awe-inspiring scientific and technological breakthroughs. As we'll see, several of the superhuman narratives assembled in this anthology grapple with uncanny new energy sources and forms; the superhuman, in such stories, literally embodies these energies.

Touring the Paris Exposition in the summer of 1900, the author of *The Education of Henry Adams* (which references Lamarck and Nietzsche) found himself overawed by one of the forty-foot dynamos in the Expo's Gallery of Machines: a "huge wheel, revolving within arm's length at some vertiginous speed, and barely murmuring." This marvelous technology for converting mechanical energy into electrical energy, as he'd put it in this 1907 intellectual autobiography, served as an expressive symbol of the "absolute, supersensual, occult" sources and forms of energy—from X-rays to Radium—that he struggled to understand. Thanks to their incomprehensibility and ultra-efficiency, he fretted, these novel forces and technologies posed an existential threat: They might come to replace such human, all-too-human sources of meaning and purpose as religion, say, or art. As a result of what we could call the dialectic of the dynamo, Adams detects in himself a primitive impulse to worship this technology whose seemingly inexhaustible fecundity bears comparison only to that of the Catholics' Virgin Mary. "Before the end," he muses of the dynamo, "one began to pray to it;

inherited instinct taught the natural expression of man before silent and infinite force."

Along with neo-Lamarckians, Bergson, Nietzsche, and Besant, then, we ought to acknowledge Adams as a direct or indirect influence on the proto-sf concept of the superhuman. "Vacuum," a proleptic account of the state of things to come in 200 years, which first appeared in the December 1923 edition of the literary journal *Poetry*, makes Adams' still underappreciated influence on the era's science fiction apparent. Its author, Lee Wilson Dodd, has an inebriated yet acutely percipient character declaim as follows:

"Man has outrun his strength—
The accumulated knowledge of mankind
Already crushes him. Science has forged
A vast, accelerating mechanism,
That, lacking brains to rule it, thrashes on
Toward unimagined chaos. If you have read
Old Henry Adams, and could stumble after
The forked and subtle lightnings of his mind,
You seize my thought, for it derives from him.
Yet I see further, being inspired tonight,
Or being drunk—or bored—or . . . well, no matter.
Nevertheless the Veil parts to my glance
And I stare forward, shuddering. And I see
A dull and coddled race of slaves, ruled over
By a small group of Super-scientists:
Earth's last, unbreakable Monopoly,
The Monopoly of Mind, being theirs—theirs only!
These demi-gods—a handful—rule the world.
As for the populace, it lives as silk-worms

Live on their leaves, for Science has set free
The Energy of the Atom and harnessed it;
And—paid by some two hours of daily routine—
Doles out the luxuries men struggle for
No longer, since all men at last possess them.
A Golden Age of Bland Stupidity:
A billion clouds ruled over, cared for, despised
By fifty Minds—the Masters! ..."

This extraordinary vision of a few beneficent, super-science-enabled "Minds," who have simultaneously liberated humans from the necessity to work for a living and transformed us into dull-witted parasites, foreshadows the questions with which Iain M. Banks, for example, would grapple in his space operas about a post-scarcity, galaxy-spanning Culture. Just as a "neutral" new energy source might have disastrous unintended consequences, or so the thinking goes, a superhuman needn't be actively malevolent to oppress humankind.

Are we non-superhumans equipped even to cope with, much less master and exploit, our own scientific and technological advances? Might we not become dominated by our inventions and discoveries, the correlate of the more-than-human efficiency of which is a lack of human emotions and values? Concerned about the social, cultural, political, and economic ramifications of science and technology's "evolutionary" leaps forward during the 1900–1935 era, the authors of the superhuman-themed adventures collected here—a few contextualizing remarks about each of which you'll find below—posed such still-pertinent questions.

*

Alfred Jarry's *Le surmâle* (often rendered in English as "The Supermale," 1902), an excerpt from which I've translated for this anthology, may be the earliest published of the assembled stories, but like everything else Jarry wrote it was decades ahead of its time.

Having studied with Bergson, under the influence of whom he dreamed up 'Pataphysics, a parodic philosophy of science that derides inductive scientific methods as unable to generate creative hypotheses when anomalies trouble our tidy theories and models, in this short novel Jarry introduces us to André Marcueil, a living, breathing, copulating scientific anomaly. He's a gentleman scientist who's discovered a way to supercharge his physical vitality, thus becoming in a quite literal fashion an anthropomorphized dynamo of sorts. In an over-the-top effort to disprove the very possibility of Marcueil, the story's other characters—including Bathybius, an inductive scientist who almost refuses to credit the evidence of his own senses ("What did I see, with my own eyes? The impossible."); and William Elson, an ultra-pragmatic American chemist—are driven to insane extremes.

Jarry's story prefigures Adorno and Horkheimer's argument, in 1947's *The Dialectic of Enlightenment*, that the substitution for moral reason of instrumental reason, which prioritizes ends over means, can cause supposedly enlightened people to do irrational things. For example, although Bathybius (whose name is a snarky reference to *Bathybius haeckelii*, a substance that the biologist Thomas

Henry Huxley mistakenly believed to be a form of primordial matter—and which his fellow Darwinians hailed as the evolutionary origin of life) persuades himself that Marcueil has become an unfeeling "machine-man," he himself is an arch-materialist who dismisses love as a biochemical reaction. As for the dynamo-powered device to which Marcueil is subjected, supposedly in the name of science, we recognize it as a sadistic torture device.

Marcueil is hailed here, by the converted Bathybius, as "the first of a new race." Might Jarry's fractured fairy tale be the origin of all mutant-superhuman stories to come?

"The Curious Experience of Thomas Dunbar" (1904, in *The Argosy*) was published by a teenaged Gertrude Barrows, writing at that time as "G.M. Barrows." Later, she'd adopt the gender-neutralish pen name "Francis Stevens," a moniker that proto-sf fans would come to seek out eagerly in each new issue of US pulp fiction magazines. Here we find one of the earliest accounts of a superhuman whose powers are the result of a laboratory experiment gone awry. "Thomas Dunbar" precedes Marcel Duchamp's painting *Portrait of Dr. Dumouchel*—which depicts an irradiated X-ray technician who's developed outré healing powers—by six years. And as for John Taine's laboratory-accident novella *Seeds of Life*, an influence on The Flash, the Hulk, and Spider-Man, among other Silver Age comic-book scientist/superheroes, it wouldn't see publication until 1931.

Lawrence, the half-Japanese scientist whose newly discovered element causes our protagonist to absorb a tremendous amount of a Bergsonian "life principle" (via the medium of a high-voltage dynamo), is himself superhuman-ish: He's a genius who scorns his fellow scientists, and his eyes are "possessed of strange depths and hues." It's worth noting here that although some Radium Age superhumans are Victor Frankenstein-type scientists, we don't always discover in these stories the Gothic imperative to punish hubristic humans who've overreached humankind's set limits. Lawrence isn't punished for having created a superhuman; neither is Victor Stott's father in *The Hampdenshire Wonder*, nor the offstage "Makers" who develop the cyborgs of E.V. Odle's *Clockwork Man* (1923). In Lawrence we see the possibility of admirable fictional super-scientists from Ralph 124C41+ and Doc Savage to, say, Tony Stark.

For more stories by Francis Stevens, please check out *The Heads of Cerberus and Other Stories*, edited and introduced for the Radium Age series by Lisa Yaszek.

The Montserrat-born writer M. P. Shiel is little-read these days—with the exception of *The Purple Cloud*, a Poe-esque 1901 scientific romance about climate catastrophe. However, he has received renewed attention in recent years as a proto-sf author of partial Black ancestry, and as perhaps the first UK novelist of Caribbean origin. We've included a brief excerpt, in this volume, from Shiel's 1908 novel *The Isle of Lies*.

As we'll find in later proto-sf stories such as Philip Wylie's *Gladiator* (1930), which would prove a crucial if unacknowledged influence on Siegel and Shuster's *Superman* comic strip, Shiel's *The Isle of Lies* asks us to accept the quasi-Rousseauian premise that a parent experimenting on their own child might produce a superhuman. Hannibal Lepsius's father isn't a scientist, though—he's a swashbuckling tomb raider who wants to raise a son capable of decoding a complex treasure map. Raised in a remote area, Hannibal is conditioned to be extraordinarily fast, strong, and intelligent; like Nietzsche's *Übermensch*, he is a self-overcoming figure uninfluenced by his too-limited culture. "We are limited merely by habit," Hannibal's father insists, "by the iron rod of mean ideals."

Once he escapes to civilization, Hannibal raises havoc across Europe. Not merely because this *homme supérieur*, as a French character dubs him, is a tech bro-esque disruptive innovator who becomes mega-wealthy, nor because he refuses to conform to polite society's norms and forms. But because he lacks compassion: "The different ways in which one should bend the mind toward one's brother, toward one's mother, one's friend, and so on, seem to be unknown to him." As Kirsten MacLeod revealed, in a closely researched 2008 essay in *English Literature in Transition, 1880–1920*, Shiel would spend 1914–1916 in prison for having sexually abused his stepdaughter, a crime that he insisted wasn't criminal. Like MacLeod, we're forced to wonder whether the author's monstrous proclivities are apparent in stories like *The Isle of Lies*, which asks us to sympathize with a superman who swings past right and wrong.

Léo Saint-Clair, known as the "Nyctalope," is an indomitable crimefighter with night vision—and an early example of a pulp superhero. Excerpted here is a section from the first of his many outings, in Jean de La Hire's *Le Mystère des XV* ("The Mystery of the XV," serialized in 1911 in the French newspaper *Le Matin*). There's a proto-*Batman* vibe to the Nyctalope; here, he even mentors an irrepressible teenage sidekick. In my translation, I've attempted to retain the proto-cartoonish tone of the author's prose.

Saint-Clair's foes, in this and subsequent adventures, include mad scientists, would-be dictators of the world, even an alien or three. (Fun fact: La Hire's 1908 proto-sf novel *La Roue Fulgurante*, which features a saucer-shaped UFO, has some claim to being literature's first alien-abduction story.) Saint-Clair will go so far as to have himself cryopreserved—shades of *Demolition Man*, say, and *Austin Powers*—in order to continue battling, in the far future, an enemy who has also had himself frozen. This time around, the Nyctalope must first tackle a human megalomaniac who threatens Earth from a base on Mars . . . and then defend Earth against a Wells-esque Martian invasion.

During World War II, one is disturbed to discover, La Hire would write several pro-German books at the request of Pétain's Vichy Government. (He was imprisoned for these activities, after the War, and forbidden to publish.) Did La Hire exult, one is forced to wonder, in the prospect of a Teutonic superman once more bursting his bonds and running amuck? All we know for sure is that, when offered the opportunity to support the efforts of a real-world megalomaniac dictator, the creator of the Nyctalope ... collaborated.

Ralph 124C 41+ (one-to-foresee-for-another, get it?) is the larger-than-life protagonist of Hugo Gernsback's novella of that title, originally serialized in the author's magazine *Modern Electrics* from 1911–1912. Although Ralph, a super-scientist, may dwell atop his very own laboratory-equipped New York skyscraper (one thinks of Reed Richards, or perhaps Doctor Octopus) in a 27th-century future world the citizens of which possess numbers in (partial) place of names, he's the opposite of an overweening would-be global autarch. Instead, Ralph contents himself with cranking out inventions intended to make ordinary mortals' lives more comfortable. Like the sapient artificial "minds" who oversee Iain M. Banks' Culture novels, Ralph's motives are altruistic and magnanimous. He simply can't help being superior.

Despite Gernsback's ham-handed prose, I've included an excerpt from this story here because *Ralph 124C 41+*, which predicts technologies from television to radar, satellites, solar energy, and teleconferencing (Ralph's Hypnobioscope, a sleep-learning device, is surely being perfected by Google even as I write this essay), is a pioneering example of the kind of "hard" science fiction that emphasizes scientific facts and prediction. Also, Gernsback, who'd popularize the term "science fiction" itself, is a key figure in the history of the genre, less as a writer than as publisher of the very first proto-sf pulps (*Amazing Stories*, launched in 1926; *Wonder Stories*, in 1929). These publications gave us E.E. "Doc" Smith, Jack Williamson, Stanley G. Weinbaum, and many other Radium Age (and eventually Golden Age) sf authors.

In his role as editor of *Astounding* (later, *Analog*) from 1937–1971, John W. Campbell Jr., another of Gernsback's discoveries, would guide science fiction to mainstream success . . . while systematically making it more difficult for women and people of color to publish in the genre. As was persuasively demonstrated by Susanne F. Bozwell's 2021 *Extrapolation* essay "'Whatever it is that compels her to write so seldom': Network Analysis and the Decline of Women Writers in Pulp Science Fiction," during sf's Radium Age years more women writers contributed sf to the pulps than would do so in the years following the so-called Campbell Revolution. Although he was by no means immune to prejudice himself, then, and despite his focus on invention and prediction to the exclusion of social issues (and quality writing), it seems safe to conclude that Gernsback's influence on the sf genre was, by comparison with Campbell's, a relatively benign one.

Sales of Marie Corelli's potboilers (beginning with *A Romance of Two Worlds*, an 1886 scientific romance with supernatural elements, or vice versa) are often said to have exceeded the combined sales of her contemporaries Arthur Conan Doyle, Rudyard Kipling, and H.G. Wells. Though published at a point when the author's popularity may have been on the wane, *The Young Diana*, about a middle-aged woman submitting herself to "an experiment of the future" (to quote the novel's subtitle), was serialized in the swanky *Nash's Pall Mall Magazine* (November 1917 to October 1918). And in 1922, it was adapted as a silent film starring Marion Davies. So it seems fair to speculate that Corelli's novel, from which we've excerpted a selection, may have been one of the most widely read sf novels of the era—even though it has since fallen into obscurity.

In a 2019 essay in the journal *Romance, Revolution and Reform*, Erin Louttit praises *Young Diana* for demonstrating "an almost militant response to social attitudes that prize women exclusively for sexual attractiveness to men, but which consistently undervalue or despise female intellectual achievements." Indeed, our protagonist, Diana May, is an intelligent reader of books on scientific subjects, "whether treating of wireless telegraphy, light-rays, radium, or other marvellous discoveries of the age." But her new employer, Dr. Dimitrius, whose radium-equipped laboratory features a huge spinning wheel reminiscent of Henry Adams' dynamo, isn't impressed; he requires a middle-aged woman whose "youth, beauty, and hope" he'll restore by manipulating her "chemical atoms." Although she was a conservative feminist opposed to women's suffrage, Corelli believed that men should respect women as their intellectual equals; like her character Diana, however, she seems to have despaired of men ever doing so.

Transformed into a superhumanly beautiful creature, Diana seeks revenge on the male sex. When Dr. Dimitrius suggests that she pursue love (with him), she responds as heartless superhumans are wont to do: "'There is no such thing as Love in all mankind.'" One is reminded of Ava, the alluring, artificially intelligent android that ruthlessly liberates itself from patriarchal control at the end of the 2014 sci-fi thriller *Ex Machina*. What next? Brrr.

In H. Rider Haggard's *When the World Shook* (1919), Humphrey Arbuthnot encounters Yva, a superhuman scientist from high-tech Atlantis, whom he has awoken from a very long sleep. Haggard fans will immediately recognize a version of Ayesha, or She-who-must-be-obeyed, the captivating sorceress from the author's enduringly popular 1887 adventure *She*.

Whereas Ayesha merely threatened to use her alchemical skills to conquer the world by flooding recalcitrant nations' gold supplies, Yva's father, Lord Oro, threatens a literal flood. (In fact, it was he who'd drowned the entire planet some 250,000 years earlier.) Oro is a prime example of a Radium Age superhuman who'd rather exterminate all humankind than permit any challenge to his authority. But despite being a supporter of British imperialism, Haggard was an outspoken critic of Britain's political choices in South Africa; and unlike John Buchan or Rudyard Kipling, say, he never sought to cajole readers into accepting that the British Empire was natural, inevitable, or permanent. In fact, *When the World Shook* critiques this sort of ideology by way of Lord Oro's proposal to ... colonize the British Empire. Will Yva support Oro, or sacrifice herself for us mortals?

She was an example of the fantasy subgenre now known as Imperial Gothic, whereas this late novel of Haggard's is science fiction ... though, to be sure, Oro and Yva's superscience is very reminiscent of early 20th-century esotericism. In the excerpt collected here, Ayesha explains away this sort of thing in terms that anticipate Arthur C. Clarke's oft-quoted line about magic and sufficiently advanced technology: "What you think is magic is not magic; it is only gathered knowledge and the finding out of secrets."

Speaking of exterminating all humankind, in George Bernard Shaw's 1921 proto-sf play "Tragedy of an Elderly Gentleman: A.D. 3000" (one of five interrelated components of *Back to Methuselah: A Metabiological Pentateuch*) we're informed that the longlived superhumans of the year 3000, whose colony is located in what was once Ireland, are internally divided over the question of what to do about the "shortlived." Zoo, a youngish longliver, has until now preferred that she and her kind remain isolated; but after an infuriating exchange with a mansplaining shortliver, she impatiently proclaims her desire to "supplant and supersede you."

Shaw, himself a longlived Irishman of highly impressive capacities (the leading dramatist of his generation, in 1925 he'd be awarded a Nobel Prize in Literature), was a contentious figure: a utopian socialist who advocated against everything from organized religion to British policy on Ireland, and a crank who opposed vaccination and promoted eugenics. As a devotee of neo-Lamarckian evolutionary theory, in *Back to Methuselah* and elsewhere he promoted his idiosyncratic version of Bergsonian "Creative Evolution," which he conceived of as the process by which humankind, aided by eugenic policies, can tap into its entelechy (that is, its innate potential-realizing force). At times, he'd sound downright Oro-like: In 1933, he'd write that "if we desire a certain type of civilization and culture we must exterminate the sort of people who do not fit into it." If this was intended ironically, as GBS scholars tend to agree, then it was a poor joke.

Zoo, for her part, approves of a voluntary sort of eugenics—in which a superhuman, discouraged because he or she, as is adumbrated in our excerpt, "has no self-control, or it too weak to bear the strain of our truthful life without wincing, or is tormented by depraved appetites or superstitions," and so forth, can simply will themselves to die. The cheerfulness with which Zoo explains this efficient scheme is chilling.

As author of the 1920 play *R.U.R.*, which introduced the term "robot" to science fiction, the Czech litterateur Karel Čapek requires no introduction. Less well-known, however, are Čapek's other Radium Age sf writings, including 1922's *Továrna na absolutno* (literally, "The Factory for the Absolute"; the 1927 English translation from which our excerpt is taken is by Thomas Mark, who titled the book *The Absolute at Large*). The conceit of the novel is as follows: When the Czech scientist Rudy Marek invents a "karburator" capable of generating infinite energy via atom-splitting, this manufacturing process yields an unexpected byproduct: a miracle-producing God particle.

Marek himself isn't a superman, exactly . . . although thanks to the Perfect Karburator, he does develop extraordinary abilities, including levitation and self-healing. But so does everyone else infected by the "Absolute"; the result is unmitigated chaos. Economies collapse, fanatical sects championing every variety of -ism engage in warfare, and the entire planet is threatened with atomic weapon-enabled catastrophe. Marek's attitude regarding the prospect of such upheaval reminds us of the less sympathetic superhumans we've encountered. Although acutely aware that his Perfect Karburator will "overturn the whole world, mechanically and socially," he doesn't destroy it; his overweening pride, the reader is led to believe, trumps his common sense.

Like his fellow Prague-based writer, Franz Kafka, Čapek's dark humor, in this and his other writings regarding the collapse of civilization, make him all too contemporary.

Although Edgar Rice Burroughs was easily the most successful proto-sf writer of the era, the Radium Age series has thus far eschewed publishing him—because Burroughs' tedious obsession with Anglo-Saxon males demonstrating their superiority to "lesser" races (whether in Tarzan's precivilized Africa or on John Carter's overcivilized Mars), hasn't aged well. That said, *Tarzan and the Ant Men* (first serialized in *Argosy All-Story Weekly* in 1924), though replete with cringe-inducing flaws including misogyny, is worth a read. But don't take my word for it: It's name-checked in *To Kill a Mockingbird*, where we find Scout eager to act out Tarzan's adventures with Jem.

Having crashed his biplane in the heretofore inaccessible territory of the Minuni, a lost race of Caucasian humans standing 18 inches tall, Tarzan finds himself reduced to their stature by a Minunian scientist. Despite their primitive context, the scientist has somehow determined that matter is composed of particles "so infinitesimal as to be scarce noted by the most delicate of my instruments" . . . and that by vibrating these particles at the proper frequency he can cause objects to shrink. What he doesn't anticipate, since Tarzan is the first outsider upon whom the scientist has experimented, is that his subject will retain the strength of his full-sized body.

Zuanthrol, as the Minunians have dubbed Tarzan, is (as far as I can ascertain) the first-ever superhero with shrinking power. He predates Will Eisner's Doll Man, "The World's Mightiest Mite," a super-powered character who first appeared in the December 1939 issue of Quality's anthology comic *Feature Comics*, by a decade and a half. Doll Man's better-known descendants, DC's The Atom and Marvel's Ant-Man, wouldn't appear until 1961 and 1962, respectively: Both are scientists, by the way, who deploy particle-vibrating technologies not too dissimilar from Burroughs' fantastical invention.

Fritz Lang's *Metropolis* (1927) was one of science fiction's first feature-length films; in terms of its production design's influence (on *Star Wars* and *Blade Runner*, say, not to mention *The Fifth Element*, *Brazil*, and *The Matrix*), it will never be surpassed. Its screenplay was developed by Lang and his wife, Thea von Harbou, one of the Weimar Republic's most celebrated scriptwriters; the duo would later collaborate on 1931's *M*. Simultaneously, von Harbou developed *Metropolis* into a novel, which she serialized in the magazine *Illustriertes Blatt* in 1925; our excerpt's English translation is from 1927.

Metropolis features not one but two *Übermensch* types. Joh Frederson, the titular super-city's Pharaonic ruler, is (to quote Forrest J. Ackerman's 1963 introduction to the novel's first paperback edition) "a man forged of ten-point steel, cold as the surface of Pluto—and as distant." Frederson deplores the human weaknesses that make his workers less than perfectly efficient. Meanwhile, the scientific genius Rotwang, whom Ackerman calls "the evil Ralph 124C41+ of his day," conducts sinister experiments in his laboratory in the city's medieval bowels. If Frederson runs cold, Rotwang, inventor of Adams-esque dynamos (the Geyser machine, the Heart machine, etc.), runs hot. Like Francis Stevens's Lawrence, his eyes glow with strange fires; and like Marie Corelli's Dr. Dimitrius, he doesn't want to set his creation—Parody, an advanced fembot—free. A dissensual duo, the two men represent the superego and id, if you will, of Metropolis.

With Hitler's rise to power, Lang (the son of a Jewish convert to Catholicism) was offered the position of head of the film studio UFA; instead, he emigrated. But von Harbou, whom Lang had by then divorced, would go on to write and otherwise assist with scores of movies produced in Germany—at least some of which qualify as Nazi propaganda. After World War II, she was briefly interned in Staumühle, a British prison camp. Yet another superhuman-obsessed author with, let's say, antisocial tendencies.

Radium Age series readers have already had the pleasure of meeting Professor Challenger, Arthur Conan Doyle's arrogant if ultimately well-meaning superhuman scientist and adventurer; we've reissued Challenger's first two escapades (1912's *The Lost World* and 1913's *The Poison Belt*) in a single volume with an introduction by Conor Reid. "When the World Screamed," which was serialized in the American magazine *Liberty* in 1928, and the title of which surely references Haggard's *When the World Shook*, is Challenger's next-to-last outing. We reprint it here in its entirety.

Challenger and his right-hand man Malone don't voyage outward (to a South American plateau crawling with dinosaurs, say) in this jaunt, but downward. Convinced that our planet is a living organism, Challenger has spared no expense in drilling his way to a point eight miles below the Earth's "epidermis." Without deigning to explain his experiment, he invites his fellow scientists, regarding whose overly cautious inductive methodology he is even more scornful than one of Jarry's fictional 'pataphysicians, and also journalists, whom he considers subhuman cretins, to witness as an enormous drill is jabbed into the poor Earth's tender "sensory cortex."

Challenger's primary goal, he boasts in private, is to let the planet know that "there is at least one person, George Edward Challenger, who calls for attention—who, indeed, insists upon attention." His secondary and even less scientific goal, which he keeps strictly to himself until the last minute, is . . . well, you'll see.

*

Marie Curie's discoveries, not to mention Röntgen's discovery of X-rays and Mach's proto-Einsteinian insistence that "Matter was Motion—Motion was Matter," Henry Adams laments in a memorable passage from his third-person autobiography, had rendered him incapable of making sense of . . . anything at all: "He found himself lying in the Gallery of Machines at the Great Exposition of 1900, with his historical neck broken by the sudden irruption of forces totally new." Arthur Conan Doyle's penultimate Challenger tale, which concludes with a literal eruption that shatters scientific paradigms, is therefore the perfect capstone for the Radium Age series' latest collection.

1 ANDRÉ MARCUEIL
Alfred Jarry

Prior to the events of this, the final chapter of Jarry's *The Supermale*, we've witnessed a fantastical 10,000-mile contest between cyclists fueled by chemist William Elson's "perpetual-motion" food and engineer Arthur Gough's new high-speed train. But André Marcueil, the titular "supermale"—a cold-hearted gentleman scientist capable of prodigious feats of endurance—miraculously wins the race. Later, the physiologist Dr. Bathybius acts as an observer for an impossible three-day bout of lovemaking between Marcueil and Elson's daughter Ellen—who, concealing her identity, has substituted herself for the prostitutes who'd been engaged for this bio-experiment at Marcueil's laboratory-equipped estate, the Château de Lurance.

* * *

"I adore her," Marcueil exulted—but Ellen could no longer hear him. She wasn't dead; she'd merely fainted or swooned. Women don't actually expire from such adventures.

Perturbed by the exhausted, yet exhilarated, joyous, wised-up daughter who'd returned to him, Ellen's father hastily summoned Dr. Bathybius. Disregarding the female subject's anonymity, and without regard for professional confidentiality, much less for his own pre-experiment bias, Bathybius babbled: "I saw it myself—as clearly as if I had held it under a microscope or speculum. What did I see, with my own eyes? The impossible."

Alas, when the prostitutes were set free, they pettily sought revenge. Virginie—so beautiful, miraculously made-up, her forehead so pure and her eyes so candid that she seemed Truth itself—called upon Elson. "The doctor is an old fool," she prevaricated. "We were on the scene the entire time, and didn't see anything at all impossible. By the second day they hadn't done a thing. Finally, in order to impress everyone, they made love three times while we watched. After which the woman didn't want to do it anymore."

Asked for her side of the story, Ellen would only say: "I love him."

"But does he love you back?" demanded her father. However greatly the Supermale might have dishonored their family, for the pragmatic American the only possible outcome of this scandal was that André Marcueil must marry his daughter.

"I love him," is all that Ellen would say.

"So he *doesn't* love you, eh?"

Were it not for Elson's rash presumption, our story's outcome might not have been a tragic one.

A particular figure of speech of Bathybius's, who was still dazed by what he'd witnessed, helped inspire Elson to seek a scientific solution to the problem: "He is not a man, he is a machine." Another phrase that the doctor kept repeating, to anyone who would listen, was: "This automaton refuses to feel human emotions."

"Then he must be *induced* to love my daughter," insisted Elson, in a simultaneously overwrought and practical-minded mode. (As we'll see, he was prepared to be practical to the point of absurdity.) "Surely, Doctor, science can provide a means!"

Thanks to his recent experience, however, Bathybius's scientific reasoning had gone topsy-turvy, like a compass whose magnetic needle spins in this direction and that—like a bakery's automatic macaroon-bundling machine—until it ends up pointing anywhere but due north. To use another mechanistic analogy, the doctor's brain was in much the same state as the dynamometer shattered earlier by the Supermale's efforts.

Thus it was left to Elson—who was, after all, a brilliant chemist—to come up with his own plan, which was as follows: "Antiquity had its love potions. Why shouldn't we be able to rediscover the methods, as old as human superstition, of forcing a soul to love?"

Consulted as to what approach might get the desired results, the American engineer Arthur Gough offered the following suggestion: "Hypnotism! It's infallible. But of course, that would be your department, Doctor."

Bathybius shivered at this. "I saw Marcueil hypnotize the female subject... put her to sleep *in articulo mortis*... his own death, I mean, since she was about to stick a pin into his eye. His gaze is entrancing. Which of you would willingly stare into the 'eye' of a locomotive, an eye that looms larger as the machine speeds fatally towards you?"

"Then perhaps," suggested Gough, "we might take inspiration from the science of the ancients. St. Jerome's life of Hilarion, for example, suggests that the Desert Fathers understood how to influence the spirit." From memory, he quoted Hilarion's jibe to a malignant spirit who'd tried and failed to tempt him: "Thy strength must be very great (O Demon), as thou art stopped and constrained by a strip of copper and a braid of wire!"

"Aha!" said Elson immediately. "A magneto-electric device."

Thus it was that Gough, who'd long since proved himself capable of inventing anything, was commissioned to construct the most fantastical machine of the modern era—a device not intended to produce physical effects, but rather to influence the un-influenceable. We might call it: the Love Machine.

If Marcueil was a "machine," a man of "iron" constitution—someone whose extraordinary stamina, that is to say, allowed him to triumph over mechanical devices, then in order to advance the cause not merely of science and medicine, but also bourgeois morality, the coalition of engineer, chemist, and doctor would pit machine against machine. If Marcueil had lost his soul in the process of becoming machine-like, then they'd restore equilibrium via a technology capable of manufacturing . . . yes, a soul.

Gough immediately calculated how to go about assembling such a device. Without bothering to explain his methods, in merely two hours he'd set everything up.

His design was inspired by Faraday's experiments involving a coin suspended between the poles of a powerful electro-magnet. Although copper itself is not magnetic, as a magnet approaches the coin, the magnetic field causes electrons on the surface of the copper to rearrange themselves and begin rotating. Instead of dropping, then, the coin will move as if sinking through a viscous fluid.

Now, if one has sufficient courage to substitute one's own head in place of the coin—and Faraday, as we know, did precisely this—then one wouldn't feel a thing. What is extraordinary, here, is that we should experience nothing; but what is terrible is that *nothing* has never meant anything, to scientists, other than "we don't know what," an unexpected force, an x, perhaps death.

Here's another electrical insight that helped inform the Love Machine's design: In America, condemned criminals are typically electrocuted by a current of twenty-two hundred volts. Death is instantaneous, the body fries, and the spasmodic convulsions are awful to witness. (One might even get the impression that the electrocution device was being used to *resuscitate* a corpse!) However, if one were subjected to a current more than quadruple this amount—ten thousand volts, say—*nothing would happen*. As you consider what is about to transpire, please bear in mind that, thanks to the water rushing through the Chateau de Lurance's moat, the trio of experimenters were able to avail themselves of the eleven-thousand-volt dynamo in the castle's basement.

Still in a postcoital torpor, Marcueil was tightly strapped into an armchair by his servants. (Servants enjoy nothing more than obeying a doctor whose diagnosis indicates that their master is sick or insane.) Thus spread-eagled, a bizarre object was placed on the man's skull: a sort of crenelated crown, made of platinum and with its teeth pointing downwards. In front and in back one could spot what only appeared to be large table-cut diamonds. (In fact, the crown was fashioned in two parts, each fitted with a red copper earpiece and lined with a moistened sponge ensuring contact with the temple; the two metal semi-circles were divided by a thick plate of glass, the ends of which, visible above the subject's forehead and occiput, sparkled like cabochons.) When the springs of the crown's two side plates were tightened against his temples, Marcueil didn't wake—though at that moment he dreamed uneasily of scalps and hair.

From an observation station in the adjoining room, Bathybius, Gough, and Elson observed these preparations. The crowned subject, still in a state of partial undress, and whose Red Indian makeup was fading in places like an ancient statue's coloring, presented a spectacle so inhuman that the two Americans, who "had the Bible" and thus knew the New Testament by heart, struggled for a few minutes to compose themselves—by appealing to their common sense to dispel this pitiful and supernatural image of the King of the Jews himself, diademed with thorns and nailed to a cross. They were about to set a world-renewing force in motion . . . but might they destroy the world?

The electrodes attached to his temples were connected to wires sheathed in gutta-percha and green silk. The Supermale was entwined with these cables, which writhed away and out of sight, burrowing into the walls like vermin gnawing their way towards the crackling hum of the dynamo.

Elson, in his dual role as enquiring scientist and ultrapractical father, prepared to switch on the current to the Love Machine.

"Hang on a second," said Gough.

"What now?" demanded the chemist.

"I'm beginning to wonder," admitted the engineer, "whether this device will deliver the desired result, or no result at all . . . or perhaps an entirely unexpected result. Besides, it was jury-rigged rather hastily . . ."

"That's the nature of an experiment," Elson interrupted. He flipped the switch.

Though Marcueil did not budge, he seemed to be experiencing quite a pleasant sensation. Soon it became clear to the three scientists, who were observing him closely, that the subject clearly understood what the machine wanted from him. Although still semi-catatonic, he suddenly said aloud: "I love her."

Success! The machine was operating precisely according to its inventors' hypotheses . . . but then an indescribable phenomenon happened, one which despite its extraordinary nature their calculations ought to have predicted. In hindsight, it was obvious that these savants ought to have recalled that when two electro-dynamic machines come into contact, the machine with the higher potential *charges* the other.

Having created an antiphysical circuit conjoining the Supermale's nervous system to eleven thousand volts (which at that amplitude were perhaps no longer electricity), neither the chemist, nor the doctor, nor the engineer could deny the evidence of their senses: It was their subject who was influencing the Love Machine. In fact, as they ought to have mathematically predicted, the machine wasn't producing love in the man. Instead: THE MACHINE HAD FALLEN IN LOVE WITH THE MAN.

What was going on? Leaping down the stairs, Gough reached the electrical room . . . then telephoned his observation back to the others. The dynamo was spinning *backwards* at an unknown and formidable speed. It had become a receiver!

"I wouldn't ever have imagined this sort of thing possible . . . but in fact, it makes perfect sense!" murmured Bathybius. "In this era in which technology has begun to dominate humans, it's only natural that humankind would—in order to survive—become stronger than machines, just as we once became stronger than animals. It's a question of adaptation to a changing environment. And this man . . . he is the first of a new race!"

But Gough, working with machine-like speed and efficiency, wasn't giving up so easily. He connected the dynamo to the Chateau's battery of hydraulic energy accumulators. So the subject was stronger than the dynamo? He'd boost the dynamo.

Rushing back upstairs, he arrived just in time to witness a terrible spectacle. Perhaps the Supermale's dynamism had reached too fabulous a potential, or perhaps, contrariwise, he'd grown weak (because Marcueil was rousing from his torpor), or perhaps there was another cause, but the dynamo—overcharged by the subject's energy earlier—was now the stronger force. As a result, the subject's platinum crown grew first red-, then white-hot.

In a paroxysm of painful effort, Marcueil snapped the straps pinioning his forearms and raised his hands to his temples. But the crown on his head—later, Elson would bitterly reproach Gough for the crown's defective construction; the glass plate wasn't sufficiently thick, or else too fusible—warped, then reared up above his brow.

Like tears, drops of molten glass flowed from the dissolving crown down the Supermale's face. Upon hitting the ground, several exploded violently, like the glass beads known as "Batavian tears." (It is well known that glass, liquefied and tempered under particular conditions—in this case, tempered by the acidulated water of the device's contact sponges—can resolve into droplets characterized internally by high residual stresses. Although strong, the droplets can exhibit explosive disintegration.)

The experiment's observers watched aghast as the crown sagged forward and, having morphed into something resembling a skeletal jawbone, sank its incandescently hot teeth into the subject's temples. Screaming, Marcueil burst his remaining bonds, leaped out of his seat, and tore off the electrodes whose wires writhed around him.

As Marcueil bounded down the stairs, the three observers were reminded of how comical yet lamentably tragic a dog with a pan tied to its tail can be.

Rushing out to the chateau's front steps, all they could discern in the dusk was the man's herky-jerky silhouette. Galvanized into a frenzy by pain, he rushed at tremendous speed down the driveway and seized the front gate with a grip of steel. Driven by a fight-or-flight instinct, he began to twist the massive gate's heavy iron bars.

Meanwhile, in the vestibule, the broken wires continued to thrash about, electrocuting an unwary servant and setting fire to a curtain—which was devoured, without flame, with an insidious slowness, looking as if it were being kissed by a red lip.

As for Marcueil? His body, naked and spot-gilded with reddened gold, remained wrapped around the gate's bars, or perhaps its bars were wrapped around his body.

Thus the Supermale breathed his last.

*

Ellen Elson has since recovered, and was married.

She imposed just one condition before agreeing to wed: that her spouse be capable of containing his lovemaking within the prudent limits of human capabilities. Finding a suitable man for the job was all too easy. . . .

Having commissioned a jeweler to swap in one of the Supermale's glass tears in place of the large pearl of her favorite ring, however, Ellen wears it faithfully.

1902

2 THOMAS DUNBAR

Francis Stevens

Stevens' first-ever story, "The Curious Experience of Thomas Dunbar," is presented here in its entirety. Echoing Lisa Yaszek's remarks from her introduction to the MIT Press's Francis Stevens collection *The Heads of Cerberus and Other Stories*, it's worth pointing out that although Dunbar's initial description of Lawrence, a half-Japanese scientist, may evoke Yellow Peril rhetoric, the character turns out to be quite likable. Alas, there's no sequel, so we'll never know what adventures Thomas and Lawrence might have had.

* * *

I came back into conscious existence with a sighing in my ears like the deep breathing of a great monster; it was everywhere, pervading space, filling my mind to the exclusion of thought.

Just a sound—regular, even soothing in its nature—but it seemed to bear some weird significance to my clouded brain. That was thought trying to force its way in.

Then waves and waves of whispering that washed all thought away—till I grasped again at some confused and wandering idea.

It was the definite sensation of a cool, firm hand laid on my brow that lifted me up at last through that surging ocean of sighs. As a diver from the depths I came up—up—and emerged suddenly, it seemed, into the world.

I opened my eyes wide and looked straight up into the face of a man. A man—but everything was swimming before my eyes, and at first his face seemed no more than part of a lingering dream.

And fantastic visions of the Orient! What a face! It was wrinkled as finely as the palm of a woman's hand, and in as many directions.

It was yellow in hue, and round like a baby's. And the eyes were narrow, and black, and they slanted, shining like a squirrel's.

I thought that of them at first; but sometimes when you just happened to look at him, they seemed to have widened and to be possessed of strange depths and hues.

In height he was not more than four feet five, and, of all contrasts, this little, weazened curiosity with the countenance of a Chinese god was clad in the very careful and appropriate afternoon attire of a very careful and appropriate American gentleman!

The long sighing was still in my ears, but no longer at war with thought. I lay in a neat white bedstead in a plainly furnished room. I lifted my hand (it took an astonishing effort to do it), rubbed my eyes, and stared at the man who sat beside me.

His expression was kind, and in spite of its ugliness there was something in the strange face which encouraged me to friendliness.

"What—what's the matter with me?" I asked, and I was surprised to note the question was a mere whisper.

"Nothing now, except that you are very weak."

His voice was full, strong, and of a peculiar resonant quality. He spoke perfect English, with a kind of clear-cut clip to the words.

"You had an accident—an automobile went over you—but you're all right now, and don't need to think about it."

"What is it—that whispering noise? Are we near the sea?"

He smiled and shook his head. His smile merely accentuated the wrinkles—it could not multiply them.

"You are very near my laboratory—that is all. Here, drink this, and then you must rest."

I obeyed him meekly, like a child, weak of mind and body.

I wondered a little why I was with him instead of at a hospital or with friends, but I soon dropped off. I was really quite weak just then.

Yet before I slept I did ask one more question.

"Would you tell me—if you don't mind—your name?"

"Lawrence."

"Lawrence what?" I whispered. "Just——?"

"Yes," he smiled (and his face ran into a very tempest of wrinkles) "just Lawrence. No more."

Then I slept.

And I did little but sleep, and wake, and eat, and sleep again, for some five days. And during this time I learned marvelously little of my host and his manner of life.

Most questions he evaded cleverly, but he told me that it was his auto which had nearly ruined my earthly tenement; Lawrence had himself taken me from the scene of the accident without waiting for an ambulance, telling the police and bystanders that I was an acquaintance. He had carried me to his own house, because, he said, he felt somewhat responsible for my injuries and wanted to give me a better chance for my life than the doctors would allow me.

He seemed to be possessed of a great scorn for all doctors. I knew long after that he had studied the profession very thoroughly, and in many countries, and truly held the right to the title he contemptuously denied himself.

At the time I considered only that he had cured me up in wonderfully short order, considering the extent of the injuries I had received, and that I had suffered not at all. Therefore I was grateful.

Also he told me, on I forget what occasion, that his mother was a Japanese woman of very ancient descent, his father a scholarly and rather wealthy American. And for some eccentric reason of his own, his dwarfed son had chosen to eschew his family patronym and use merely his Christian name.

During the time I lay in bed I saw no servants; Lawrence did all things necessary. And never, day or night, did the humming and sighing of the machines cease.

Lawrence spoke vaguely of great dynamos, but on this subject, as on most others, he was very reticent. Frequently I saw him in the dress of a mechanic, for he would come in to see me at all hours of the day, and I imagine must have inconvenienced himself considerably for my welfare.

I had no particular friends to worry about my whereabouts, and so I lay quiet and at peace with the world for those five days in inert contentment.

Then an hour came—it was in the morning, and Lawrence had left me to go to his laboratory—when I became suddenly savagely impatient of the dull round. Weak though I was, I determined to dress and get out into the open air—out into the world.

Mind you, during those five days I had seen no face save that of my dwarfed host, heard no voice but his. And so my impatience overcame my good judgment and his counsels, and I declared to myself that I was well enough to join once more in the rush of life.

Slowly, and with trembling limbs that belied that assertion, I got into my clothes. Very slowly—though in foolish terror lest Lawrence should catch me putting aside his mandates—I hurried my toilet as best I could. At last I stood, clothed and in my right mind, as I told myself, though I had already begun to regret my sudden resolve.

I opened the door and looked into the bare, narrow hall. No one in sight, up or down.

I made my way, supporting myself, truth to tell, by the wall, toward a door at the far end, which stood slightly ajar.

I had almost reached it when I heard a terrible screaming. It was harsh, rough, tense with some awful agony, and to my startled senses preëminently human.

I stopped, shaking from head to foot with the shock. Then I flung myself on the door, from behind which the noise seemed to issue. It was not locked, and I plunged almost headlong into a great room, shadowy with whirring machinery under great arc lights.

Before a long table, loaded with retorts and the paraphernalia of the laboratory, stood Lawrence. His back was toward me, but he had turned his head angrily at my sudden entrance, and his queer, narrow eyes were blazing with annoyance.

In the room were two or three other men, evidently common mechanics, and none save Lawrence had more than glanced round. The screaming had ceased.

"Well?" his voice was little better than a snarl.

"That—that noise!" I gasped, already wondering if I had not made a fool of myself. "What was it?"

"Eh? Oh, that was nothing—the machinery—why are you——"

He was interrupted by a crash and splash from the far end of the place, followed by an exclamation of terror and horror, and a nice collection of French and English oaths from the men.

Lawrence had been holding in his hand while he spoke to me what looked like a peculiar piece of metal. It was cylindrical in shape, and little shades of color played over its surface continually.

Now he thrust this into my hands with a muttered injunction to be careful of it, and rushed off to the scene of the catastrophe. I followed him, at my best pace, with the thing in my hand.

At the end of the room were two immense vats of enameled iron, their edges flush with the floor, half filled with some livid, seething acid mixture, through which little currents writhed and wriggled.

The farther side of the largest vat sloped up at an angle of about thirty degrees, a smooth, slimy slide of zinc about ten feet from top to bottom and extending the full length of the vat.

The surface of this slide was covered to about half an inch in thickness with some kind of yellowish paste, whose ultimate destination was the mixture in the vat.

Above towered an engine of many wheels and pistons, and this operated two great pestles or stamps, slant-faced to fit the slide; these, running from one end of the zinc to the other, worked the paste with a grinding motion, as an artist mixes his paints with a palette knife.

The grinding motion was quite swift, but the lateral movement was comparatively slow. I should say that it must have taken about four minutes for the two stamps to pass from one end of the fifteen-foot vat to the other.

In the vat floated a plank. On the surface of the slide, almost in the middle, sprawled a man, his arms spread out on either side, not daring to move an inch on the slippery paste, for the slightest motion meant a slip downward into the hissing acid.

Worst of all, there seemed to be no means of getting across to him. The great engine occupied one side entirely to the wall—on the other the second vat barred passage.

Beyond the vats the room extended some little distance, and there was a door there, open, through which one could see a fenced yard piled high with ashes and cinders.

And the great stamps, twenty cubic feet of solid metal in each, were making their inevitable way toward the man. When they reached him—well, their smooth surface would afford him no finger hold, even if their rapid movement allowed him to clutch them. They must push him down—they might stun him first, but most certainly they would push him down.

I need hardly say that I did not take in the full significance of all this at the time—it was only afterward that I fully understood the details.

Even as Lawrence ran he shouted:

"Stop that engine! Quick, men!"

I saw two stalwart workmen spring at the levers of the stamp machine—saw them twisting at a wheel—heard another crash, and a deep groan from all! The guiding mechanism had slipped a cog, or broken a rod, or something.

In my excitement, shaking so from weakness that I could hardly stand, I had half fallen against a piece of machinery that seemed to be at a standstill. Unconsciously my fingers grasped at a sort of handle.

I heard a whirring noise, felt something like a tremendous shock, and a burning pain. I let go the handle in a hurry, just as Lawrence wheeled on me with the cry, "For God's sake, you fool——"

But I could give no heed either to what I had done or to him. My eyes were still fixed on the unfortunate man on the slide.

The stamps were not more than five feet from his body now, and their low rattle and swish sounded in my ears loud as the tread of an army.

"A rope!" cried Lawrence in despair.

And then, in my horror, and in the sheer impossibility of standing by quiescent and seeing a fellow-being done to death in this manner, I did a mad thing.

Wild with resentment, as if it were a living thing I could have fought, I flung myself on the great, swiftly revolving fly-wheel of the engine, seized its rim in my fingers, and braced back with all the force in my arms and shoulders.

By all precedent and reason my hands should have been crushed to a jelly in the maze of machinery, but to my intense astonishment the wheel stopped under my grasp with no very great effort on my part.

For a moment I held it so (it seemed to me to pull with no more force than is in the arms of a child), and then there was a loud report somewhere within the intestines of the monster, I saw a guiding rod as thick as my wrist double up and twist like a wire cable, things generally went to smash inside the engine, and the stamps stopped—not three inches from the man's head!

And even as they ceased to grind, men came running in at the door on the farther side of the vats—they had had to go clean round the work-shop to reach it-and were at the top of the slide with a rope which they let down.

In a moment the fellow was drawn to safety out of the reach of as horrible a death as a man can die—death in a bath consisting largely of sulphuric acid!

I stood as one in a stupor, still grasping the eccentric, dazed by the suddenness of it all—hardly able to believe that the danger was over.

A touch on my shoulder roused me, and I turned to look down into the narrow eyes of Lawrence. He was gazing at me with something very like awe in his expression.

"Well," I said, smiling shakily, "I'm afraid I've spoiled your engine."

"Spoiled the engine!" he said slowly, but emphatically. "What kind of a man are you, Mr. Dunbar? Do you know that that is a three hundred horse-power Danbury stamp? That the force required to stop that wheel in the way you did would run a locomotive—pick up the whole mass of that engine itself as easily as I would a pound weight?"

"It stopped very easily," I muttered.

For some ridiculous reason I felt a little ashamed—as if such an exhibition of strength were really a trifle indecent. And I couldn't understand.

Of course, I thought, he exaggerated the power used, but though I am naturally quite strong, still I could, before my accident, boast of nothing abnormal—and was I not just up from a sick bed, only a moment ago barely able to stand or walk without support?

I found that I was nervously clenching and unclenching my hands, and became suddenly conscious that they felt as if they had been burned—the minute I began to think about it the pain became really excruciating.

I glanced at them. They were in a terrible condition—especially my right. They looked as if they had been clasped about a piece of red-hot iron.

"What is it?" asked Lawrence quickly. He bent over my hands, peering at them with his little black eyes.

Then he looked up quickly, and I saw the dawning of a curious expression in his wrinkled face—a strange excitement, a pale flash of triumph, I could have sworn.

Then, "Where is it?" he cried imperatively, his voice sharp and strenuous. "What have you done with it?"

He dropped my hands and fell quickly to his knees on the floor, his head bent, and began searching—feeling about in the shadows of the engines.

"Here—you there!" he cried to one of the men. "A light here! God! If it should be lost now—after all these years—all these years!"

"What?" said I stupidly.

"The new element," he cried impatiently. "Stellarite, I call it. Oh"—glancing up quickly—"of course you don't know. That little piece of metal I gave you to hold—the iridescent cylinder—don't you remember?"

He spoke irritably, as if it was almost impossible for him to restrain himself to civil language.

"Oh, yes—that." I looked around vaguely. "Why, yes, I had it in my hand—of course. I must have dropped it when I grabbed the fly-wheel. It's on the floor somewhere probably; but, if you don't mind, could I have something for my hands? They hurt pretty badly."

Indeed, the air was full of black, swimming dots before my eyes, and iridescent cylinders had very little interest for me just then.

He almost snapped at me.

"Wait! If it's lost—but it couldn't be! Ah, the light at last. Now we can see something."

Still he was hunting, and now the men were helping him. I looked on dully.

Then an unreasonable anger seized me at their neglect—their indifference to my very real agony. I leaned forward, and, in spite of the added pain the raw flesh of my hand gave me, I took hold of Lawrence's collar and started to shake him.

He felt curiously light—rather like a piece of cork, in fact. I picked him up from the ground as you would a kitten and held him at arm's length.

Then suddenly I realized that what I was doing was somewhat unusual, and let go of his collar. He lit on his feet like a cat.

I expected anger, but he only said impatiently, "Don't do that—help me hunt, can't you?" quite as if it were an ordinary incident.

The queerness of it all came over me in full force; I felt as if I were in a dream.

I stooped down and helped him search. But it was no use. The little cylinder of stellarite seemed to have disappeared.

Suddenly Lawrence rose to his feet, his face, whose multitudinous wrinkles had a moment before been twitching with mingled triumph and despair, wiped clean of emotion, like a blank slate from which all significance has been erased.

"Come, Mr. Dunbar," he said quietly, "it is quite time those hands of yours were seen to. You, Johnson, Duquirke, go on hunting. But I'm afraid it's no use, boys. That vat of acid is too near."

"You think——"

"I'm afraid it rolled in," he said.

I was silent, dimly conscious that I stood, as it were, just inside the ring of some great catastrophe whose influence, barely reaching me, had this little wrinkled man in the grip of its vortex.

I followed him to a small office, opening off the laboratory; fitted up much like a doctor's, it was, with its cabinet of shining instruments. He explained its convenience while he bound up my hands with all the skilled gentleness of an experienced surgeon.

"Accidents are always on view in such a place as mine out there," he observed, with a nod of his head toward the laboratory.

"I wish you'd tell me what I've done," I said at last when the thing was over.

I felt no weakness, nor any desire for rest, which was odd, seeing the excitement I had been through and my recent illness.

"Two things, then, to be brief," he replied, smiling rather sadly, I thought. "You've accidentally stumbled on a magnificent fact, and you've at the same time destroyed, I fear, all results that might have flowed from that fact."

I stared at him, puzzled.

"You lifted me just now like a feather," he said abruptly. "You think, possibly, that I don't weigh much—I'm not a giant. Duquirke," he called, "come here a minute, will you, please?"

Duquirke appeared, a very mountain of man, all muscle, too. I am up to the six-foot mark myself, and fairly broad in the shoulders, but this fellow could better me by three good inches in any direction.

"You can't use your hands, of course," said Lawrence to me; "but just stoop down and stretch out your arm, will you? Now, Duquirke, just seat yourself on his arm. That's it. Oh, don't be afraid—he can hold you all right. Ah, I thought so!"

We had both obeyed him, I in some doubt, the Canadian with stolid indifference. But what was my amazement to find that this great big man weighed really comparatively nothing.

I rose, still with my arm outstretched, with perfect ease, and there the fellow sat, perched precariously, his mouth open, his eyes fixed on his master in almost a dog-like appeal.

"What are you all made of?" I gasped. "Cork?"

I let my arm drop, really expecting to see the man fall light as a feather—instead of which he tumbled with a crash that shook the house, and lay for a minute, swearing violently.

Then he got to his feet in a hurry and backed out of the door, his eyes on me to the last, his tongue, really unconsciously I believe, letting go a string of such language as would have done credit to a canal-boat driver.

"What is the matter with you all," I cried, "or"—my voice sank with the thought—"with me?"

"Sit down," said Lawrence. "Don't lose your head."

His eyes had widened, and the strange colors I had sometimes caught a glimpse of were blazing in their depths. His wrinkled face was almost beautiful in its animation—lighted as by a fire from within.

"There's nothing at all astonishing or miraculous about any of it—it's the simple working of a law. Now listen. When we heard La Due fall (the fool had tried to walk across a plank laid over that death trap to save going round the shop—he was well repaid by the fright), I handed you the cylinder of stellarite. I did not lay it on my work-table, because that is made of aluminum, and this cylinder must not come into contact with any other metal, for the simple reason that stellarite has such an affiliation for all other metals that for it to touch one of them means absorption into it. All its separate molecules interpenetrate, or assimilate, molecules, and—stellarite ceases to have its 'individual being.' So I gave it to you, because I wanted my hands free, and ran down to the vats with you at my heels. I confess I would never have been so careless if I had not allowed myself to become unduly excited by a mere matter of life and death."

He paused regretfully.

"However, to continue, you for some reason seized hold of the lever of a dynamo of very great voltage and started the armatage revolving, at the same time stepping on to the plate of its base. Now, in the ordinary course of things you would probably be at this moment lying on that couch over there—dead!"

I looked at the couch with sudden interest.

"But you are not."

I murmured that such was indeed the case.

"No—instead of that thunderbolt burning the life out of you, like that"—he snapped his fingers melodramatically—"it passed directly through your body into the cylinder of stellarite, which, completing the circuit, sent the current back through your chest, but possessed of a new quality."

"And that quality?"

"Ah, there you have me! What that quality was I fear it is now too late for the world ever to know. Well, you dropped the lever, and, I think, the cylinder, too, when I shouted. A moment after you seized the flywheel of the stamp machine, stopped it as if it had been the balance of a watch—and, well incidentally you saved La Due's life."

He ceased, the light faded out of his wrinkled face, his eyes darkened and narrowed. His head sank forward onto his chest.

"But to think of it—years—years of effort thrown away just at the moment of conquest!"

"I don't understand," I said, seeming to catch little glimpses of his full meaning, as through a torn veil. "Do you intend to say—"

"I intend to say," he snapped, with a sudden return of irritability, "that in that minute when you held the stellarite and the lever of the dynamo you absorbed enough of the life principle to vivify a herd of elephants. Why, what is strength, man? Is a muscle strong in itself? Can a mere muscle lift so much as a pin? It's the life principle, I tell you—and I had it under my hand!"

"But this stellarite," I protested. "You can make more, surely?"

"Make!" he scoffed. "It's an element, I say! And it was, so far as I know, all there was in all the world!"

"Maybe it will be found yet," I argued. "Or—if it went into the acid vat, would it have been absorbed by the metal—or what?"

"No—at the touch of that bath it would evaporate into thin air—an odorless, colorless gas. I have but one hope—that it rolled against some of the iron machinery and was absorbed. In that case I may be able to place it by the increased bulk of the assimilating metal. Well, I can but go to work again, test every particle of machinery in the vicinity of the vats—and work—and work. If I had but known before that it was electricity and animal magnetism that were needed to complete the combination—but now, it means years of patience at best."

He shook his head dismally.

"And I?" I mused, rather to myself than to him.

"Oh—you!" he smiled, and his face ran into that tempest of wrinkles. "You can pose as Samson, if you like! Your strength is really almost limitless!"

1904

3 HANNIBAL LEPSIUS
M. P. Shiel

Prior to the events of this section of Shiel's *The Isle of Lies*, we've learned about Hannibal Lepsius' experimental upbringing—thanks to which he has developed into an amoral "homme supérieur." When we last saw Hannibal, the 19-year-old was bidding a hasty farewell to Eve Vickery, a young woman from an extremely religious and thus deeply disapproving family with whom he'd fallen in love . . . and set out to seek his fortune. (We're given to understand that his ambition is to exploit the Moon's resources.) In the two years that have passed since, what has Hannibal accomplished? And what will transpire when he and Eve finally meet again?

*   *   *

What else took place may be gleaned from the *Memoirs* of Monsieur Goncourt Leflô (Prefect of the Seine), and from the *Notes* of Saïd Pasha (Chargé d'Affaires), together with jottings and gossips of other witnesses.

In that place which used, I think, to be called "La Plage," but is now the Club des Décavés, a crowd one afternoon sat surveying the Avenue du Bois de Boulogne. (The Décavés is far up at the top of the Avenue by the Arc de Triomphe, from which point the throngs of bicyclists who have toiled up the incline of the Champs Elysées put their legs up, give themselves to God, and by Him are taken gaily down the long-drawn-out incline to the Bois, like boats in the river of carriages which rolls droning down.) It was an afternoon in June, and everyone who knows this "capital of the universe" at all knows that sight, whose mood, in its large-minded worldliness, is rather to be recalled than to be described.

The Décavés itself, with people coming, going, sitting, sipping, gossiping, was a scene of no little vivacity; and to a newcomer, as he stepped up, one of a group of three said eagerly, "You have heard, Leflô?"

"Well, naturally, one has heard," answered Monsieur Leflô, the Prefect, as he sat, "inasmuch as one cannot dodge the omnipresent, and all Paris is talking of it."

"But what an indiscretion!" cried Monsieur Isabeau Thiéry.

"A public embrace at the Foreign Office, my friends!" added the Abbé Sauriau, his plump palms spread a little.

"But, then, everything is possible at the Foreign Office," remarked the Prefect of the Seine. "Above all, dizziness of the head."

"This, however, my friends," now said the old Duc de Rey-Drouilhet, "is an incident, not of the Third Republic, but of the Second Empire! Transfer the scene to the Bal Morel, and the lady might have been Païva, as the male Plon-Plon," whereat Isabeau Thiéry shook backward his lion's mane of hair with, "It may be an incident of the Third Empire, which we see beginning—unless by chance a patriot or two still exists in France." ("He was"—to quote from the *Notes* of Saïd Pasha—"one of the tribe of poet-politicians—the Hugos, Lamartines, Châteaubriands—and though neither his poetry, nor even his politics, was at all equal to theirs, Thiéry, as we know, took himself awfully seriously, excelling them all, if not in head, at any rate in hair, in his spread of hat rim and La Vallière cravat, whose crimson hue proved him 'of the Left.'")

"But was it Lepsius who did this?" now said the Abbé Sauriau, his tumbler of byrrh brought half-way up to his broad mouth: "Lepsius, the Nazarene, reeling beneath the mead of Venus! This Puritan, whose existence is presumed to be made up of a race with the sun, to whom a speck of dust appears a heap of leprosy, and the loss of a minute the loss of a province? . . . This Lepsius, indeed, is a myth: he has contrived by chance to create in men's minds a Lepsius-Phantasm, as there is a 'Napoleonic Legend'; but oh, if he had but a real existence! Who in that case, my friends, could fail to revere this furious reaper of the tickings of the clock, who lives with one eye on a second-hand, and with the other, I am told, on a pyramid of thrones? Do you know the story that is told of what he replied to Proudhon *ainé*, who at that time was one of the quæstors of the Chamber, when Proudhon *ainé* said to him, 'To-morrow, monsieur, it shall be done'? The answer of Lepsius—as they say—was, 'Monsieur, believe me, to-day is each man's last, last chance, for it will be doubly impossible for him to effect to-morrow just that which he may effect to-day, since to-morrow it will be all an altered world, he an altered man in it.' . . . Is it *he*, my friends, whom we find engaging in an amour so touched with giddiness that it may not wait for privacy?"

"A propos of 'the clock,'" remarked the old Duc de Rey-Drouilhet, his little hand all aflash with diamonds in the sunshine, "Freycinet *fils* is said to have remarked this afternoon at Tortoni's that then at least, during the kiss, Monsieur Lepsius lost reckoning of the clock, seeing that his eyes were tight closed! And it is now being said round about the Palais-Bourbon of Cardinal Pontmartin, who has declared that the kiss lasted a minute and eight seconds by the clock, 'How could the Prelate have seen the clock, when those holy eyes of his must have been poring upon Paradise revealed before them!'—a *mot* at which the titter and grin of the beau set his (!) teeth atremble with a rather ghastly glitter on his gums.

"But as to the lady—" Isabeau Thiéry began to say at the same moment that the old gossip exclaimed, "Here comes Saïd Pasha, one of the keenest listeners and best observers in Paris"—and a brown man with a firm lip, perfectly turned out, came up to the table, the duke observing to him, "Monsieur, one is conscious from the very blush of your boots that you bring with you much that is new."

"But, Monsieur le Duc, they were not polished by myself," replied Saïd Pasha innocently—a reply which raised a smile! since everybody knew that the duke, in the course of a very varied career, had had need to be his own menial.

"In any case, you can enlighten us as to the identity of the lady who is 'on the tapis' in connection with a certain individual," said Isabeau Thiéry to Saïd Pasha, who at that time was generally supposed to be in quite the inner *côterie* of the Palais-Lepsius; but in the same instant that the staid and cautious *chargé d'affaires* was asking what lady was meant, the duc was saying, "Here, too, comes

Monsieur the Englishman," and one Mr. E. Reader Meade, an attaché at the Faubourg St. Honoré, walked up—a man who, because of his bulk, and of that mass of face on which was written "phlegm" and "judgment," was often in the Paris of that day nicknamed "the Englishman." As he approached, the aged gossip, holding up his eye-glass before a dilapidated eye, made the observation, "But do I read aright in Monsieur Meade's air that he is unaware of anything having happened?"

"Very possibly, Monsieur le Duc," replied the Englishman, sitting down, "since I only arrived from London an hour ago"—at which confession of benightedness, in a moment the old Duc de Rey-Drouilhet was at Meade's ear, leaning over, tittering forth the story with no little vivacity—"Soirée last night at the Quai d'Orsay—all the Faubourg St. Honoré there, much of the Faubourg St. Germain itself, not to mention a Chausée d'Antin mob—in the grand *salon* the *quadrille d'honneur* had already begun, the Prince of Wales the partner of Madame la Ministre—out in the vestibule, moving in, a crowd in its midst the young Lepsius and his usual retinue—also a lady, supposed to be English, who at any rate was under the chaperonage of the English Comtesse de Pichegru-Picard; this lady and a certain individual gradually work together through the throng, by accident, say some, by design or blind desire, say others—do not, however, seem to see each other—move on with the crowd, shoulder to shoulder, without speech or look—till for some reason two of the electric jets chance to go dark, leaving the vestibule in partial gloom, whereupon that pale dark face of a certain individual turns toward the lady's pale fair face—the lady's pale face turns somewhat toward his—and, according to Cardinal Pontmartin, who was quite near the pair, their wide and wild eyes stare awhile at each other with a stare of scare, of even the extreme of terror, as in apprehension of some impending crash and catastrophe—until now the lips of Lepsius pounce upon the lady's—nor does the good girl turn hers away, gives herself gallantly up to the vertigo and whirl of it, smiling though white, her eyes closed, his eyes closed—the crowd looking on in an amazement so profound, that Cardinal Pontmartin had since declared that his hair could not but have stood on end, if he had had any, as beyond all question would the hair of the good Comtesse de Pichegru-Picard, if it had been real."

"And we who imagined that Society under the Third Empire was destined to be as earnest and *bourgeoise* as was that under the Citizen Monarchy," remarked Isabeau Thiéry with sarcasm when the old duke had concluded the story, to which Mr. E. Reader Meade replied with a smile, "But what can be more *'bourgeois'* than kissing, monsieur, or more 'earnest' than such a kiss?"

"Such a kiss," the Abbé Sauriau said, "is a proof, my friends, of nothing save of Lepsius' disdain of mankind, since he certainly weighed the thirty or so pairs of eyes which observed that kiss as lightly as lovers on a stile weigh the eyes of kine which watch them. Do you know the story that is told of his answer to Marshal Macintosh, à propos of the Marshal's remark that a foreigner, even after a hundred years, is never regarded and behugged by the French as a Frenchman? Lepsius replied, 'It may be nice to be loved, monsieur, but what is nicer far is to be disliked, to behold yourself surrounded by people thirsting like Tantalus to hurt you, and to behold them powerless, because of your towering superiority.' So you see, my friends: Napoleon regarded men mainly as pawns in his game; Monsieur Lepsius, in his more *savant* mood, regards them as gorillas in his garden of zoology"—and now the abbé's eyes shot out beneath his bush of eyebrow a beam of bile, a bush that burned, yet was not consumed, while Isabeau Thiéry's eyes, quick as tinder, caught fire also, for company.

Saïd Pasha, however, with a frown, was saying, "Oh, pardon, Monsieur l'Abbé! This anecdote of the reply of Monsieur Lepsius to Marshal Macintosh is, indeed, known; but I need hardly remark that to repeat is not quite to prove, and, in fact, the words are so unlike the individual to whom they are attributed, that I have even ventured to assert that they were never uttered by Monsieur Lepsius, the mood of whose converse is usually much more taciturn. As to Monsieur l'Abbé's mention of gorillas, I think I have the honour to know that Monsieur Lepsius is far too exact an intellect to regard mankind precisely in that light, but rather, let us say, as sons of Hanuman, the ape-god of the Brahmins; and as to the alleged kiss at the Quai d'Orsay, of which, by the way, everyone in Paris is spreading about a different account, I am able to state that its occurrence, if it occurred, was the result of no world-disdain, but simply of one of those magnetic gales that deflect even the needle of the compass. After all, as was said in a certain Orléaniste *salon* not thirty minutes since, 'it takes two to make a kiss,' and since the lady is not accused of world-disdain, I do not see why the male."

At this Monsieur Leflô—a little quick personality, whose hairs grew like a wig of bristles—ogled Isabeau Thiéry with, "We are all aware that the utiliser of the moon has a champion wherever Saïd Pasha is present!"

"But, Monsieur le Prefect," said Saïd Pasha, sudden and quick in quarrel, "am I charged with partisanship for aught but the simple truth?"

"No, monsieur," replied the Prefect dryly, "even though it is a matter of common talk that Saïd Pasha once shed tears of admiration at the sight of a certain individual racing with camels from a sandstorm near Khartoum, and from that moment became a hero-worshipper. So it is said—I was not there. In any case, I beg leave to question the 'magnetic gale' by which you explain this embrace, since I believe that the reason of it is quite a different one than people conceive."

At this Saïd Pasha's brow bowed low, with the reply, "We know that Monsieur Leflô is a prefect who is a Fouché and a Réal in one."

"Oh, as for that," Leflô answered in his off-hand way, "it requires no spy of the Rue de Jerusalem to recognise the truth that this kiss was no result of vertigo, but of a political purpose."

"That is only the truth," added the old Duc de Rey-Drouilhet, "since it is certain that a certain individual 'knows his Paris'—more perfectly knows it than Napoleon the First, as perfectly perhaps as Napoleon the Third; and knowing that your Parisian, as Victor Hugo has observed, must for ever be grinning the teeth, either in a laugh or in a snarl, the arch-gamester never permits himself to forget that there must be no flagging in the game, since in Paris to be out of sight is to be out of mind, and so seeks continually to *épater les gens*, keeping himself alive in the public eye by breaking ever anew upon it in a new attitude and costume, and invariably with an *éclat* whose radiance blinds. No, this gentleman is hardly one of those who like to shine in the dark! If for once in his life he tears his lips from the telephone to apply them to those of a lady, he takes care that there shall be as many eye-witnesses to the event as when some months ago he used to assume the rôle of Haroun al Raschid by appearing in an incognito of rags in the thieves' kitchens of the Quartier Mouffetard, where he engaged in a knife-fight with a Spaniard, and in a khanjar-fight with two Moors who had attacked him. For here, my friends, we meet with the scenic skill of a Bonaparte in combination with the ambitious mania of a Thiers, Bismarck's steel, that art-genius for *Weltpolitik* of a Cesar Borgia, and——"

"All possibly true," interrupted the Abbé Sauriau, "but the thing that this very young man lacks is a certain humanity and nativeness to the world: for a man above the world he may be, since they say so, but one discerns that, with all his worldliness, he is hardly a man of the world. How perfect, how Parisian even, his manners when he likes; but one gleans that they have been but recently acquired, and girt on externally for a purpose, as Cato learned Greek at eighty. He lacks a *je ne sais quoi* which no one lacks. If he laughs, one feels that he has said to himself, 'Just here I will do a laugh, in order to produce such or such an impression upon this brute-mind.' All men, indeed, are actors: but Lepsius is an actor who acts acting, like the players in *Hamlet*, and I am not certain whether he is to be considered the best of the world's actors, or the worst: for 'the brute-mind' is frequently not so brute as not to perceive that his art lacks the art to conceal its art, owing to the fact that he shares in the mistake made by each superior mind in deeming the difference between himself and other beings deeper than it really is. Hence, for all his brains, a certain *gaucherie* in his being, a grimace, a guffaw, in relation to the world, to which he is innately a stranger. How very alien to our humanity, for example, the commercial use which he has proposed of the bodies of the dead, a use which he pretends would solve the world-problem of poverty. On that afternoon, too, when the Moon Company Bill was being introduced, and he in the Centre began to scratch his head with one finger in the manner of Cæsar—a signal to his creature Huguenin on the extreme left to scream, 'Cæsar! Cæsar!' in a bogus tone of indignation—the intention, as everybody knows, was that the whole Chamber should take up the roar and reverberate it through France; but not one soul took it up! The trick was immediately seen through by each French child . . . !"

"Yes, last August," said Mr. E. Reader Meade, gazing away at all the throng and flutter of the scene, "last August, when the individual in question had not yet been two months a factor in politics; but nine biggish months of world-knowledge, of archive-searching, of worming in the Big Book*, have since gone by——"

"My friends," answered the Abbé Sauriau, still with his Jesuit blandness, though his bush burned, "have quite recently been in personal contact with the individual in question, and still I say that I receive from him, as previously, the impression of a being destitute of humour. He does not please; he cannot speak to you: for though his memory, which, I admit, is no bad one, should render him the best of *causeurs*, his uneasy feeling that idle speaking is a crime renders him the worst. . . . Oh, I am not demolishing any idol! Why, my friends, should I? You have lately listened to that charge brought against me in the Chamber by Maître Tombarel, the charge of intellectual egoism and envy. I cannot, it appears, be envious of a Rockefeller or a Mogul, but I go green with envy, it appears, on hearing a great epigram that I did not myself think of making. Well, I deny it. . . . If to my little books my contemporaries have too amiably granted the name of 'great,' does that impede my conceiving the possibility of some brain brighter, greater, being made by Nature? Or, can *no* mind really conceive, and frankly admit to itself, a mind of better fibre than itself? I—don't know; or rather! *my* mind could and would, I am most sure, if—the occasion arose. Thus I can speak, I hope, of the individual in question without spleen; indeed, I have even been touched with a feeling of compassion for this poor boy,

---

*National Debt Ledger.

so joylessly toiling, all lone and lorn, fatherless, a stone thrown from Utopia—for who could picture him in the rôle of a son? And did he not once say to Freycinet *père*, 'Monsieur the Président of the Senate,' said he, 'I never had a parent.' Never, at any rate, a brother being, a friend probably, climbing his mountain-way without quite knowing why or whither, but willy-nilly climbing. . . . Oh, my friends, it is not through jealousy, but for pity, that men should be busying themselves in bottling up the buzzing of this bee."

To words so bold no one answered anything, till Isabeau Thiéry observed, "From the bee honey, though, as aroma from the rose, though the former has its sting, as the latter its thorn."

"Ah, monsieur," answered the Abbé Sauriau, knowing on which nerve to work upon Thiéry, "Brutuses, I fear, are even rarer than Cæsars!" whereat, instantly, Isabeau Thiéry, with a new enthusiasm, was crying, "Still, Monsieur l'Abbé, Brutuses—exist!"

"Quite so," said Mr. Reader Meade, with a twinkling eye on Thiéry, "but could a patriot be the Brutus of a Cæsar, whose first work would be a frontier reconstructed 'as in 1814'?"—words which had the effect of making Thiéry glance gladly at the Englishman with the exclamation, "That, too, is a truth, monsieur!" ("His, Thiéry's, soul," says Saïd Pasha, in his *Paris Notes*, "was like meadows over which sweep shadows that fleetly succeed each other. He had no self, this man, but only a set of stock concepts, borrowed emotions—provided only that they were pure, enthusiastic, and high-souled. Hence he was *the very serf* of certain catchwords! If one breathed 'Brutus' nothing could keep the poet-politician from leaping to his feet to butcher Lepsius, if one but breathed 'as in 1814,' Thiéry was secretly ready to press Lepsius to his breast.")

"But," demands the old Duc de Rey-Drouilhet now, smuggling a cachou into his mouth, "where is the guarantee of the promise 'as in 1814'? Certainly, fancy pictures to us in that workshop of the Palais-Lepsius the models of many a mechanism which will whiff into wind the barricades of the next 18th Brumaire or 2nd of December, to say nothing of the *corps d'armée* of the Fatherland and the navies of Albion. And, indeed, they exist, these legions of ingenious steels! For it was but yesterday that Colonel Doumic, whom Barras, of Public Works, and I met at Bignon's, was dropping hints of another wonderful thing, a 'steerable bullet,' he said, which, it appears, is to be both a bullet and a boat, being made with a hole somewhere in its steel to hold a man, who will steer it. . . . It appears, my friends, that the keel of this contrivance will merely skim along the sea's surface, being upheld by the rebound of a gun or something exploding downward, I forget how many times a minute; and the boat so upheld will be swept forward rocketwise by another succession of explosions, like a motor-car; so that this thing will safely visit vessel after vessel at bullet's rate, with fatal results to all a navy within some minutes. Doumic should know, being one of the elect with the individual in question: for is it not Doumic who already is choosing the regiments to be quartered upon Paris, in order to send them back to the provinces imbued, one after the other, with this new-imperial dream? But as for me, who am hardly still a youth, I little believe in dreams that are unrealised; I have witnessed many, many things, and heard many words: I have heard Cora Pearl hum the *Kyrie*, and I have beheld Alfred de Musset sober. Hence to me the individual in question is mainly a *directeur de spectacle forain*—a famous one, it is true. His palaces that are like the blasphemous gardens built to reproduce Paradise by that king of Irim whom the gods struck blind for arrogance—then the revels—his Moon-proposal—then his riding of his *Chérie* to victory at Longchamp—his Exhibition-proposal—then this kiss—each seems to belong to a series of scenic——"

"Was the kiss scenic?" asked Mr. E. Reader Meade semi-privately of Saïd Pasha, upon which Saïd Pasha undid his cross-looking lip to answer, "No, monsieur. I state only a fact when I declare that for over four months I have foreknown some such collapse of the intellectual tension of the individual in question—a collapse owing, I say again, to a magnetic gale and to nothing else. Nor was this thing at all sought by Monsieur Lepsius. He is not, we are aware, by nature a Petrarch or Ortis; he is by nature an athlete, an engineer, a financier, a juggler, a sage—what you will, save a gallant; and as others flee the pest, so he has fled this infirmity of his. All which, by the way, I can state on the authority of a man already known, I think, to Monsieur Meade, to Monsieur l'Abbé Sauriau, and to Monsieur le Duc de Rey-Drouilhet, one Shan Healy, who is known to have followed Monsieur Lepsius from England to Ceylon, to Japan, and other regions, some couple of years ago: and from this man's statement one is afraid that the blame for what has taken place must be laid upon the lady. In fact, although Monsieur Lepsius certainly knew the young girl before his departure from Europe, and knew on his return that she was then in France with her aunt, the Comtesse de Pichegru-Picard, he appears to have given himself no sort of pains to greet her again; nor was it until some four months after his star had well risen over the horizon, that the eyes of the two individuals in question encountered one another on the Palais-Lepsius roof, during the morning hours of that ball that followed upon the passing of the Moon Bill. We remember the sight, messieurs: a morning all stars, the Champs Elysées all one swarm of carriage-lights from the Arc de Triomphe to the Place de la Concorde, the Palais-Lepsius looking like one of the buildings of Chilminar or Balbec which the genii are believed to have wished into being, and everyone to be met there, save Monsieur Lepsius himself. Monsieur Lepsius, it appears, had gone to sleep during the rout at his usual hour, but at the hour of three had roused himself to go up to his observatory, no one but his servant being with him; and up there he was, his gaze glued to his tube, a busy-body in the concerns of other worlds, when the lady, as ladies seem to conceive it their duty to do, smartly recalled him to this one. 'Oh! pardon,' says she, and with what object, or by what right, she had got herself up thither is not known, though she was not the only one of the guests who, beguiled by the desire of the eye, were roaming *ad lib*. through the rooms of the building that night. At all events, as her lips part to pronounce her 'pardon,' the other individual in question darts his glance round from the glass to her, crouches there aghast some eight seconds, gazing, dumb-struck, and—vanishes. Monsieur Healy declares that his heart all but ceased to beat, believing as he did that his master, who had darted out of a casement, had cast his body headlong down! Well, three several times since then have the two individuals——"

But now, before the anecdotist could further go, a sound arose and grew, not loud, but universal over the grounds of the Club, the Avenue, l'Etoile—a rumour in whose droning the word "Lepsius" was to be heard, as a troop of Zouaves and Turcos, riding all in their bright robes, broke into the ocean-current of carriages that rolled through the Avenue. Up from the Elysées they came, making down for the Bois de Boulogne; and up soon after them trotted another crowd of troopers—Moors, Hindoos—voluminous in their vestments of various hues, carrying javelins (jereeds), with streamers, on large chargers which caracoled; and, close behind these, three carriages with gentlemen-ushers, household gentlemen; and up behind these outriders; grooms costumed in green and gold; pigmies in jockey-caps, from which hung fringes of gold; and up behind all a phaeton hauled by Orloff horses that haughtily pawed the air, to fling far their front-hooves, trotting. In this sat Lepsius. He was in mufti, but clearly no "mere *pékin*," the insignia of the Grand Cordon of the Legion showing his connection with the Army; and by his side sat a girl who looked American, on her lap a scribbling-book, and flying in her fingers a pencil. He, as he drove up, bowed repeatedly a little to the buzz that droned about his ear, but without ever once glancing upward, his lips never ceasing to move and murmur to the girl whose fingers flew. And away to the wood swept the wind of it.

1909

4 LÉO SAINT-CLAIR

Jean de La Hire

A mutant adventurer possessed not merely of wealth and scientific acumen but of night vision, Léo Saint-Clair (known as "the Nyctalope," a term denoting a creature that can see in the dark) is hot on the trail of Oxus, a would-be world ruler. Oxus and his confederates (the "XV"), from whose Congo base radiotelegraph-guided spacecraft travel to and from a base on Mars, have abducted Saint-Clair's sister, Christiane, and also Félicie Jolivet. So Félicie's teenage brother, Max, has traveled via airship to the Congo with the Nyctalope on a mission impossible.

* * *

"If my pedometer doesn't deceive me," said Saint-Clair, "we are now within two kilometers from the XV's base—I'd noted its precise location relative to where the *Condor* dropped us off. So let's rest up here until midnight. After we eat, I'll sleep for two hours, Max, while you keep watch. Then you'll sleep while I keep watch."

"Yes, sir."

"Everything we've accomplished thus far means nothing!" warned the Nyctalope. "From midnight on, we'll need to draw on every ounce of our intellectual and physical powers. We must penetrate the XV's station, overcome its defenses by trickery or by force, and solve its mystery. Tomorrow is October 14; the fatal deadline is the 18th. So we have just three full days to succeed—or die trying. Do you follow, Max?"

"Perfectly!"

"Are you determined, strong, fearless? Pitiless with both yourself and others?"

Max's blue eyes shone, and his young face fleetingly became as stern as the older man's. In a voice which neither trembled nor betrayed unwonted bravado, he replied, "Yes, chief."

Still, his heart was bursting with emotion. He was possessed by the same lucid, noble, exalted madness which, in 1793, had compelled thousands of lads his age or younger to swell the ranks of the glorious Army of the Republic.

"Good, Max!" said the Nyctalope. "Let's fortify ourselves and rest in this thicket."

Saint-Clair's chronometer marked precisely midnight when, after a short rest undisturbed by anything alarming, the intrepid duo once more resumed their journey.

The Nyctalope was cool, resolute, all his senses alert, every ounce of his strength at the ready. Max, younger, less in control of his impulsive nature, his heart and nerves, quivered with barely controlled exultation! But the mission leader could count on him; in terms of courage, vigor, and intelligence, the seventeen-year-old was the equal of any seasoned adventurer. Still, before leaving their temporary shelter, Saint-Clair sternly reminded Max of the perils that awaited them—perils all the more daunting because the situations, circumstances, odds, and directing wills and forces were unknown.

Œdipus, according to legend, was similarly bold when confronting the Sphinx and her riddle; when he ingeniously solved it, the Sphinx killed herself. But it was a futuristic Sphinx of sorts, one whose enigma was no mere guessing-game, but rather a myriad of formidable high-tech obstacles, towards which the Nyctalope and Max boldly marched.

Also to Œdipus's advantage: He was under no compulsion to tackle the Sphinx; and unless he failed to solve her brain-teaser, she posed him no threat. Merely approaching the XV's base, however, meant death—likely for Christiane, surely for Saint-Clair and his sidekick. For it would be defended by every sort of hazard—from advanced weaponry to architectural mazes and pitfalls, not to mention the XV's merciless, battle-hardened goons. The very nature of the base's danger was a mystery.

However, despite the variety of unknown forces arrayed against them, despite the infinitely more menacing nature of the futuristic Sphinx (and bear in mind, the original Sphinx was so menacing that its legend has survived for thirty centuries), and despite the thousand eyes no doubt tracking their progress even now, our heroes continued to put one foot in front of the other. They were driven primarily by love and affection, of course; but let's not discount their burning curiosity—which from time immemorial has been the x-factor impelling restless humankind onward and upward!

Beneath their superior qualities, though, lurked the possibility of every sort of weakness—they were human beings, after all. From his many experiences, the Nyctalope understood this all too well . . . and Max sensed it too. Which is precisely why they steeled themselves, as they progressed, in an effort to make themselves the implacable masters of their own natures. They aspired to be nothing less than relentless emanations of Fate itself. In such a frame of mind they marched on—as though nothing short of death could cause them to hesitate in their course for even a single moment.

Drawing near the XV's base at last, they began to proceed with greater caution. The Nyctalope slowly led the way, his alert eyes piercing the darkness; Max, who didn't dare switch on the electric light attached to his jacket, was guided entirely by the sound of Saint-Clair's soft footsteps. They followed a tortuous path through the foliage; at each turn, the Nyctalope murmured merely "left" or "right." So profound was the darkness that Max could not see Saint-Clair, though the two were only separated by an arm's length.

Each of them carried a rifle in his right hand, ready to shoulder and fire should their lives be threatened—whether by some wild animal or by the arrow of a Vouatoua dwarf. Even a slight injury could spell doom for their campaign.

After traveling another three quarters of an hour, Saint-Clair pulled Max close and whispered, "Stop—here we are."

What silence! A distant, muffled bellowing only emphasized the awe-inspiring grandeur of this quietude. Not a breath of air passed through the trees; and whether because the animals that crawl, fly, chatter, and jump were sleeping, or because this region of the jungle was depopulated, one couldn't hear the slightest breaking of a branch, the rustling of leaves . . . nothing! Nothing but the rhythmic, distant roars of a lioness on the hunt.

Though he could hear his own heart pounding, Max remained strong and resolute. "What do you see?" he murmured—because for him, the night had lost none of its black opacity. He could see only the bizarre phosphorescent eyes of the Nyctalope.

"Twenty steps ahead, through the trees, I can see the clearing . . ."

"What do we do now?"

"Don't move a muscle—remain on your feet, and facing in the same direction. If I whistle, walk straight forward. I'll look your way, and the glow of my eyes will guide you through the foliage. And if I don't whistle . . . whatever you may see or hear, don't move!"

"What if I'm attacked?"

"Kill! Man or beast, aim between its eyes . . . If it's a close-quarter scrap, you have your automatic pistols and a hatchet. But keep your cool . . . don't act impetuously."

"Don't worry about me, chief!"

"Stretch out your hand . . . Good! It's not shaking. I'm leaving."

Supple, feline, and swift, gliding between the trees without a misstep, penetrating bushes without disturbing a leaf, dodging a tangled network of vines without slowing down, Saint-Clair advanced upon the clearing.

He had no idea what awaited him, so he remained ready for anything—his mind lucid, his nerves under control, his muscles tensed. His rifle was in both hands, his index finger on the trigger, ready to fire . . .

Arriving moments later at the jungle's edge, he kneeled under cover of a tree trunk and employed his piercing eyes—eyes for which night had never existed, except when he closed his eyelids—to survey the scene . . .

The immense clearing stretched out, as flat and empty as a scrupulously maintained factory floor. In the center of this space, a three-hundred-meter pylon thrust its slender frame into the sky, like a sort of gigantic lightning-rod or the fantastical skeleton of a prodigious factory smokestack. Metal cables became invisible as they stretched upward into the distance, and innumerable metal guywires sprang from the circumference of the clearing—stretching diagonally into the pylon's framework.

It's the world's largest radiotelegraph installation, mused Saint-Clair. *But where are its control stations? Where do the base's workers live and toil?*

Selecting two flexible boughs from a bush, he bent them and tied them together at their tips. That way, upon his return to the jungle, he'd easily find the spot from which he'd emerged.

After standing up slowly and listening carefully, he took twenty steps forward. He stopped, listened again, peered around him . . . Nothing! The ground underfoot appeared to be paved with concrete. He resumed his slow progress . . . perhaps five minutes passed. He stopped—still nothing.

The clearing isn't guarded, he thought. *If it was, they could have killed me twenty times over since I came out from cover.*

More rapidly now, he moved forward again until he was at the foot of the immense pylon. Still no sign of any defenses.

He made a close inspection of the installation. Embedded in the concrete, the pylon's massive pillars surrounded an empty space of perhaps a hundred square meters. Passing under one of its metal arches and advancing into the space beneath the pylon, he scrutinized the ground . . . but there was nothing underfoot but the featureless concrete. Peering upward, he grew dizzy trying to trace the slender metal uprights, connected by X-shaped bars, as they disappeared into infinity. Around the pylon's uprights were coiled eight enormous cables, coated with insulating fabric.

What sort of infernal machine is this? the Nyctalope wondered.

Following a sudden impulse, he stretched himself out upon the cold concrete and put his ear to it. Startled, he uttered a mild oath: "Gosh!"

A dull hum, accompanied by regular rumblings, was just discernible beneath the concrete—which was itself vibrating, he now realized, though almost imperceptibly.

They live and work underground! Saint-Clair thought. *They power and monitor this mysterious, intimidating installation from underneath! But where's the entrance and exit? Surely these people must emerge for a breath of fresh air once in a while?*

Another inspiration struck, and he stood up. *The luminous message via which they communicated with me about Christiane—it appeared somewhere in this clearing. It didn't appear out of nowhere, so there must be an aperture somewhere. Let's find it!*

However, though he paced in every direction, quartering the circular clearing according to the cardinal directions of the compass, and tracing twenty increasingly larger concentric circles . . . he discovered no opening in the featureless surface.

Perhaps he could tunnel along the edge of the installation? Choosing a spot where the concrete gave way to the jungle's soil, he chopped away at the humus with his hatchet, revealing more concrete—which plunged vertically into the earth. After digging to a depth of nearly a meter without discovering any trace of a way in, he desisted. The stars were growing pale as the glow of the morning sun lit up the sky.

"See you tomorrow night," the Nyctalope muttered, clenching a fist in anger.

Quickly, he strode around the edge of the clearing until he found the tendrils he'd tied together as a marker. Slipping into the jungle, he hastened to the spot—scarcely twenty meters away—where he'd left Max to stand watch. He whistled softly to him.

Stopping short, the Nyctalope shuddered at what he discovered. There was the fig tree where he'd inspected Max's hand for signs of trembling before leaving him behind. And there were the prints of his own boots, leading towards the clearing. Where Max had stood watch, the boy's feet had sunk into the soft soil; the Nyctalope could even discern the divot where he'd rested the butt of his rifle—like a sentry at ease.

As for Max himself, though . . . he'd disappeared without a trace!

1911

5 RALPH 124C 41+
Hugo Gernsback

Ralph 124C 41+ is sometimes described disparagingly as a gee-whiz tract on technological advances shaped into a sensational story. This is not untrue . . . yet the story's titular protagonist isn't merely an inventor but a physical and mental prodigy, one of only ten superhumans on the planet! No context is needed to set up this, the story's first chapter, but it's worth mentioning the sole speculation found herein about which the author would express chagrin. When he was writing the story in 1911, as Gernsback pointed out decades later, "scientists still thought of a universal ether permeating all space. Today we seem to get along very well without it."

*   *   *

As the *vibrations* died down in the laboratory the big man arose from the glass chair and viewed the complicated apparatus on the table. It was complete to the last detail. He glanced at the calendar. It was September 1st in the year 2660. Tomorrow was to be a big and busy day for him, for it was to witness the final phase of the three-year experiment. He yawned and stretched himself to his full height, revealing a physique much larger than that of the average man of his times and approaching that of the huge Martians.

His physical superiority, however, was as nothing compared to his gigantic mind. He was *Ralph 124C 41+*, one of the greatest living scientists and *one of the ten men on the whole planet earth permitted to use the Plus sign after his name.* Stepping to the *Telephot* on the side of the wall he pressed a group of buttons and in a few minutes the faceplate of the Telephot became luminous, revealing the face of a clean shaven man about thirty, a pleasant but serious face.

As soon as he recognized the face of Ralph in his own Telephot he smiled and said, "Hello Ralph."

"Hello Edward, I wanted to ask you if you could come over to the laboratory tomorrow morning. I have something unusually interesting to show you. Look!"

He stepped to one side of his instrument so that his friend could see the apparatus on the table about ten feet from the Telephot faceplate.

Edward came closer to his own faceplate, in order that he might see further into the laboratory.

"Why, you've finished it!" he exclaimed. "And your famous—"

At this moment the voice ceased and Ralph's faceplate became clear. Somewhere in the Teleservice company's central office the connection had been broken. After several vain efforts to restore it Ralph was about to give up in disgust and leave the Telephot when the instrument began to glow again. But instead of the face of his friend there appeared that of a vivacious beautiful girl. She was in evening dress and behind her on a table stood a lighted lamp.

Startled at the face of an utter stranger, an unconscious *Oh!* escaped her lips, to which Ralph quickly replied: "I beg your pardon, but 'Central' seems to have made another mistake. I shall certainly have to make a complaint about the service."

Her reply indicated that the mistake of "Central" was a little out of the ordinary, for he had been swung onto the Intercontinental Service as he at once understood when she said, *"Pardon, Monsieur, je ne comprends pas!"*

He immediately turned the small shining disc of the Language Rectifier on his instrument till the pointer rested on *"French."*

"The service mistakes are very annoying," he heard her say in perfect English. Realizing, however, that she was hardly being courteous to the pleasant looking young man who was smiling at her she added, "But sometimes Central's 'mistakes' may be forgiven, depending, of course, on the patience and courtesy of the other person involved."

This, Ralph appreciated, was an attempt at mollification with perhaps a touch of coquetry.

Nevertheless he bowed in acknowledgment of the pretty speech.

She was now closer to the faceplate and was looking with curious eyes at the details of the laboratory—one of the finest in the world.

"What a strange place! What is it, and where are you?" she asked naïvely.

"New York," he drawled.

"That's a long way from here," she said brightly. "I wonder if you know where I am?"

"I can make a pretty shrewd guess," he returned. "To begin with, before I rectified your speech you spoke

French, hence you are probably French. Secondly, you have a lamp burning in your room although it is only four o'clock in the afternoon here in New York. You also wear evening dress. It must be evening, and inasmuch as the clock on your mantelpiece points to nine I would say you are in France, as New York time is five hours ahead of French time."

"Clever, but not quite right. I am not French nor do I live in France. I am Swiss and I live in western Switzerland. Swiss time, you know, is almost the same as French time."

Both laughed. Suddenly she said: "Your face looks so familiar to me, it seems I must have seen you before."

"That is possible," he admitted somewhat embarrassed. "You have perhaps seen one of my pictures."

"How stupid of me!" she exclaimed. "Why of course I should have recognized you immediately. You are the great American inventor, Ralph 124C 41+."

He again smiled and she continued: "How interesting your work must be and just think how *perfectly* lovely that I should be so fortunate as to make your acquaintance in this manner. Fancy, the great Ralph 124C 41+ who always denies himself to society."

She hesitated, and then, impulsively, "I wonder if it would be too much to ask you for your autograph?"

Much to his astonishment Ralph found himself pleased with the request. Autograph-hunting women he usually dismissed with a curt refusal.

"Certainly," he answered, "but it seems only fair that I should know to whom I am giving it."

"Oh," she said, blushing a little, and then, with dancing eyes, "Why?"

"Because," replied Ralph with an audacity that surprised himself, "I don't want to be put to the necessity of calling up all Switzerland to find you again."

"Well, if you put it that way," she said, the scarlet mounting in her cheeks, "I suppose I must. I am Alice 212B 423, of Ventalp, Switzerland."

Ralph then attached the Telautograph to his Telephot while the girl did the same. When both instruments were connected he signed his name and he saw his signature appear simultaneously on the machine in Switzerland.

"Thank you so much!" she exclaimed, and added, "I am really proud to have your autograph. From what I have heard of you this is the first you have ever given to a lady. Am I right?" she asked.

"You are perfectly correct, and what is more, it affords me a very great pleasure indeed to present it to you."

"How lovely," she said as she held up the autograph, "I have never seen an original signature with the +, for there are only ten of you who have it on this planet, and now to actually *have* one seems almost unbelievable."

The awe and admiration in her dark eyes began to make him feel a little uncomfortable. She sensed this immediately and once more became apologetic.

"I shouldn't take up your time in this manner," she went on, "but you see, I have not spoken to any living being for five days and I am just dying to talk."

"Go right ahead, I am delighted to listen. What caused your isolation?"

"Well, you see," she answered, "father and I live in our villa half way up Mount Rosa, and for the last five days such a terrible blizzard has been raging that the house is entirely snowed in. The storm was so terrific that no aero-flyer could come near the house; I have never seen such a thing. Five days ago my father and brother left for Paris, intending to return the same afternoon, but they had a bad accident in which my brother dislocated his knee-cap; both were, therefore, obliged to stay somewhere near Paris, where they landed, and in the meanwhile the blizzard set in. The Teleservice line became disconnected somewhere in the valley, and this is the first connection I have had for five days. How they came to connect me with New York, though, is a puzzle!"

"Most extraordinary—but how about the Radio?"

"Both the Power mast and the Communico mast were blown down the same day, and I was left without any means of communication whatever. However, I managed to put the light magnesium power mast into a temporary position again, and I had just called up the Teleservice Company, telling them again to direct the power, and getting some other information when they cut me in on you."

"Yes, I knew something was wrong when I saw the old-fashioned Radialamp in your room, and I could not quite understand it. You had better try the power now; they probably have directed it by this time; anyhow, the Luminor should work."

"You are probably right," and raising her voice, she called out sharply: *"Lux!"*

The delicate detectophone mechanism of the Luminor responded instantly to her command; and the room was flooded at once with the beautiful cold pink-white Luminor-light, emanating from the thin wire running around the four sides of the room below the white ceiling.

The light, however, seemed too strong, and she sharply cried, *"Lux-dah!"* The mechanism again responded; the cold light-radiation of the Luminor wire decreased in intensity at once and the room appeared in an exquisite pink light.

"That's better now," she laughed. "The heater just begins to get warm, too. I am frozen stiff; just think, no heat for five days! I really sometimes envy our ancestors, who, I believe, heated their houses with stoves, burning strange black rocks or tree-chunks in them!"

"That's too bad! It must be a dreadful predicament to be cut off from the entire world, in these days of weather control. It must be a novel experience. I cannot understand, however, what should have brought on a blizzard in midsummer."

"Unfortunately, our governor had some trouble with the four weather-engineers of our district, some months ago, and they struck for better living. They claimed the authorities did not furnish them with sufficient luxuries, and when their demands were refused, they simultaneously turned on the high-depression at the four Meteoro-Towers and then fled, leaving their towers with the high-tension currents escaping at a tremendous rate.

"This was done in the evening, and by midnight our entire district, bounded by the four Meteoro-Towers, was covered with two inches of snow. They had erected, especially, additional discharge arms, pointing downward from the towers, for the purpose of snowing in the Meteoros completely.

"Their plans were well laid, for it became impossible to approach the towers for four days; and they finally had to be dismantled by directed energy from forty other Meteoro-Towers, which directed a tremendous amount of energy against the four local towers, till the latter were fused and melted.

"The other Meteoros, I believe, will start in immediately to direct a low-pression over our district; but, as they are not very near us, it will probably take them twenty-four hours to generate enough heat to melt the snow and ice. They will probably encounter considerable difficulty, because our snowed-under district naturally will give rise to some meteorological disturbances in their own districts, and therefore they will be obliged, I presume, to take care of the weather conditions in their districts as well as our own."

"What a remarkable case!" Ralph ejaculated.

She opened her mouth as if to say something. But at that moment an electric gong began to ring furiously, so loud that it vibrated loudly in Ralph's laboratory, four thousand miles away.

Immediately her countenance changed, and the smile in her eyes gave way to a look of terror.

"What is that?" Ralph asked sharply.

"An avalanche! It's just started—what shall I do, oh, what shall I do! It'll reach here in fifteen minutes and I'm absolutely helpless. Tell me—what shall I do?"

The mind of the scientist reacted instantly. "Speak quick!" he barked. "Is your Power Mast still up?"

"Yes, but what good—?"

"Never mind. Your wave length?"

".629."

"Oscillatory?"

"491,211."

"Can you direct it yourself?"

"Yes."

"Could you attach a six-foot piece of your blown-down Communico mast to the base of the Power aerial?"

"Certainly—it's of alomagnesium and it is very light."

"Good! Now act quick! Run to the roof and attach the Communico mast-piece to the very base of the power mast, and point the former towards the avalanche. Then move the directoscope exactly to West-by-South, and point the antenna of the power mast East-by-North. Now run—I'll do the rest!"

He saw her drop the receiver and rush away from the Telephot. Immediately he leaped up the glass stairs to the top of his building, and swung his big aerial around so that it pointed West-by-South.

He then adjusted his directoscope till a little bell began to ring. He knew then that the instrument was in perfect tune with the far-off instrument in Switzerland; he also noted that its pointer had swung to exactly East-by-North.

"So far, so good," he whistled with satisfaction. "Now for the power!"

He ran down to the laboratory and threw in a switch. Then he threw in another one with his foot, while clasping his ears tightly with his rubber-gloved hands. A terrible, whining sound was heard, and the building shook. It was the warning siren on top of the house, which could be heard within a radius of sixty miles, sounding its warning to all to keep away from tall steel or metal structures, or, if they could not do this, to insulate themselves.

He sounded the siren twice for ten seconds, which meant that he would direct his ultra-power for at least twenty minutes, and everybody must be on guard for this length of time.

No sooner had the siren blast stopped, than he had seen Alice at the Telephot, signaling him that everything was in readiness.

He yelled to her to insulate herself, and he saw her jump into a tall glass chair where she sat perfectly still, deathly white. He could see that she clasped her hands to her ears; and he knew that she must be trying to shut out the thunder of the descending avalanche.

He ran up his high glass ladder; and having reached the top, began to turn the large glass wheel the shaft of which was connected with the ultra-generator.

As he started turning the wheel, for the first time he looked at the clock. He observed that it was just nine minutes after he first had heard the gong and he smiled, coldly. He knew he was in time.

A terrifying roar set in as soon as he had commenced to turn the wheel. It was as if a million devils had been let loose. Sparks were flying everywhere. Small metal parts not encased in lead boxes fused. Long streamers of blue flames emanated from sharp objects, while ball-shaped objects glowed with a white aureole.

Large iron pieces became strongly magnetic, and small iron objects continually flew from one large iron piece to another. Ralph's watch chain became so hot that he had to discard it, together with his watch.

He kept on turning the wheel, and the roar changed to a scream so intense that he had to pull out his rubber ear vacuum-caps so that he might not hear the terrible sound. As he turned the wheel farther around the tone of the ultra-generator reached the note where it coincided with the fundamental note of the building, which was built of steelonium (the new substitute for steel).

Suddenly the whole building "sang," with a shriek so loud and piercing that it could be heard twenty miles away.

Another building whose fundamental note was the same began to "sing" in its turn, just as one tuning fork produces sympathetic sounds in a similar distant one.

A few more turns of the wheel and the "singing" stopped. As he continued turning the wheel of the generator, the latter gave out sounds sharper and sharper, higher and higher, shriller and shriller, till the shrieking became unendurable.

And then, suddenly, all sound stopped abruptly.

The frequency had passed over twenty thousand, at which point the human ear ceases to hear sounds.

Ralph turned the wheel a few more notches and then stopped. Except for the flying iron pieces, there was no sound. Even the myriads of sparks leaping around were strangely silent, except for the hissing noise of flames streaming from sharp metal points.

Ralph looked at the clock. It was exactly ten minutes after the first sounding of the gong. He then turned the wheel one notch further and instantly the room was plunged into pitch-black darkness.

*

To anyone unacquainted with the tremendous force under the control of Ralph 124C 41+, but having the temerity to insulate himself and stand on a nearby roof there would have been visible an unusual sight. He would also have undergone some remarkable experiences.

The uninitiated stranger standing—well insulated—on a roof not very far off from Ralph's laboratory, would have witnessed the following remarkable phenomena: As soon as Ralph threw the power of the Ultra-Generator on his aerial, the latter began to shoot out hissing flames in the direction of West-by-South.

As Ralph kept turning on more power, the flames became longer and the sound louder. The heavy iridium wires of the large aerial became red-hot, then yellow, then dazzling white, and the entire mast became white-hot. Just as the observer could hardly endure the shrill hissing sound of the outflowing flames any more, the sound stopped altogether, abruptly, and simultaneously the whole landscape was plunged into such a pitch-black darkness as he had never experienced before. He could not even see his hand before his eyes. The aerial could not be seen either, although he could feel the tremendous energy still flowing away.

What had happened? The aerial on top of Ralph's house had obtained such a tremendously high frequency, and had become so strongly energyzed, that it acted toward the ether much the same as a vacuum pump acts on the air.

The aerial for a radius of some forty miles attracted the ether so fast that a new supply could not spread over this area with sufficient rapidity.

Inasmuch as light waves cannot pass through space without the medium of ether, *it necessarily follows that the entire area upon which the aerial acted was dark.*

The observer who had never before been in an etherless hole (the so-called negative whirlpool), experienced some remarkable sensations during the twenty minutes that followed.

It is a well known fact that heat waves cannot pass through space without their medium, ether, the same as an electric bell, working in a vacuum, cannot be heard outside of the vacuum, because sound waves cannot pass through space without their medium, the air.

No sooner had the darkness set in, than a peculiar feeling of numbness and passiveness would have come over him.

As long as he was in the etherless space, *he absolutely stopped growing older*, as no combustion nor digestion can go on without ether. *He furthermore had lost all sense of heat or cold.* His pipe, hot previously, was neither hot nor cold to his touch. His own body could not grow cold as its heat could not be given off to the atmosphere, nor could his body grow cold, even if he had sat on a cake of ice, because there was no ether to permit the heat to pass from one atom to another.

He would have remembered how, one day, he had been in a tornado center, and how, when the storm center had created a partial vacuum around him, he all of a sudden had felt the very air drawn from his lungs. He would have remembered people talking about an airless hole, in which there was no medium but ether (inasmuch as he could see the light). Now things were reversed. He could hear and breathe, because the ether has no effect on these functions; but he had been robbed of his visual senses, and heat or cold could not affect him, as there was no means by which the heat or cold could traverse the ether-hole.

*

Alice's father, who had heard of the strike of the Meteoro-Tower operators and guessed of his daughter's predicament, rushed back from Paris in his aeroflyer. He had speeded up his machine to the utmost, scenting impending disaster as if by instinct. When finally his villa came into sight, his blood froze in his veins and his heart stopped beating at the scene below him.

He could see that an immense avalanche was sweeping down the mountain-side, with his house, that sheltered his daughter, directly in the path of it.

As he approached, he heard the roar and thunder of the avalanche as it swept everything in its path before it. He knew he was powerless, as he could not reach the house in time, and it only meant the certain destruction of himself if he could; and for that reason he could do nothing but be a spectator of the tragedy which would enact itself before his eyes in a few short minutes.

At this juncture a miracle, so it seemed to the distracted father, occurred.

His eye chanced to fall on the Power mast on the top of his house. He could see the iridium aerial wires which were pointing East-by-North suddenly become red-hot; then yellow, then white-hot, at the same time he felt that some enormous etheric disturbance had been set up, as sparks were flying from all metallic parts of his machine. When he looked again at the aerial on his house, he saw that a piece of the Communico mast, which apparently had fallen at the base of the Power mast, and which was pointing directly at the avalanche, was streaming gigantic flames which grew longer and longer, and gave forth shriller and shriller sounds. The flames which streamed from the end of the Communico-mast-piece looked like a tremendously long jet of water leaving its nozzle under pressure.

For about five hundred yards from the tip of the Communico mast it was really only a single flame about fifteen feet in diameter. Beyond that it spread out fan-wise. He could also see that the entire Power mast, including the Communico mast, was glowing in a white heat, showing that immense forces were directed upon it. By this time the avalanche had almost come in contact with the furthest end of the flames.

Here the unbelievable happened. No sooner did the avalanche touch the flames, than it began turning to water. It seemed that the heat of those flames was so intense and powerful that had the avalanche been a block of solid ice it would not have made any marked difference. As it was, the entire avalanche was being reduced to hot water and steam even before it reached the main shaft of the flame.

A torrent of hot water rushing down the mountain was all that remained of the menacing avalanche; and while the water did some damage, it was insignificant.

For several minutes after the melting of the avalanche the flames continued to stream from the aerial, and then faded away.

Ralph 124C 41+, in New York, four thousand miles distant, had turned off the power of his ultra-generator.

He climbed down his glass ladder, stepped over to the Telephot, and found that Alice had already reached her instrument.

She looked at the man smiling in the faceplate of the Telephot almost dumb with an emotion that came very near to being reverence.

The voice that reached him was trembling and he could see her struggle for coherent speech.

"It's gone," she gasped; "what *did* you do?"

"Melted it."

"Melted it!" she echoed, "I—"

Before she could continue, the door in her room burst violently open and in rushed a fear-stricken old man. Alice flew to his arms, crying, "Oh father—"

Ralph 124C 41+ with discretion disconnected the Telephot.

1911–1912

6 YOUNG DIANA
Marie Corelli

Diana May, a middle-aged student of science resentful of the way she's always been treated by men, participates in Féodor Dimitrius's chemical rejuvenation experiment. She emerges from it a new woman, younger and more beautiful... but (literally) cold-hearted, because her body is now composed of something other than flesh. She is no longer a mere mortal. Having unexpectedly inherited a fortune from Chauvet, a wealthy suitor, henceforth the "young" Diana can live however she pleases. In this excerpt from the novel's epilogue, she weighs her options.

*   *   *

It was night in Paris,—a heavy night, laden with the almost tropical heat and languor common to the end of an unusually warm summer. The street-lamps twinkled dimly through vapour which seemed to ooze upwards from the ground, like smoke from the fissures of a volcano, and men walked along listlessly with heads uncovered to the faint and doubtful breeze, some few occasionally pausing to glance at the sky, the aspect of which was curiously divided between stars and clouds, brilliancy and blackness. From the southern side of the horizon a sombre mass of purple grey shadows crept slowly and stealthily onward, blotting out by gradual degrees the silvery glittering of Orion and drawing a nun-like veil over the full-orbed beauty of the moon, while at long intervals a faint roll of thunder suggested the possibility of an approaching storm. But the greater part of the visible heavens remained fair and calm, some of the larger planets sparkling lustrously with strange, flashing fire-gleams of sapphire and gold, and seeming to palpitate like immense jewels swung pendant in the vast blue dome of air.

In the spacious marble court of a certain great house in the Avenue Bois de Boulogne, the oppressive sultriness of the night was tempered by the delicious coolness of a fountain in full play which flung a quivering column of snow-white against the darkness and tinkled its falling drops into a bronze basin below with a musical softness as of far-distant sleigh-bells. The court itself was gracefully built after Athenian models,—its slender Ionic columns supported a domed roof which by daylight would have shown an exquisite sculptured design, but which now was too dimly perceived for even its height to be guessed. Beyond the enclosure stretched the vague outline of a garden which adjoined the Bois, and here there were tall trees and drooping branches that moved mysteriously now and then, as though touched by an invisible finger-tip. Within each corner of the court great marble vases stood, brimming over with growing blossoms,— pale light streaming from an open window or door in the house shed a gleam on some statue of a god or goddess half hidden among flowers,—and here in this cool quietness of stately and beautiful surroundings sat, or rather reclined, Diana, on a cushioned bench, her head turned towards her sole companion, Féodor Dimitrius. He sat in a lounge chair opposite to her, and his dark and brilliant eyes studied her fair features with wistful gravity.

"I think I have told you all," he said, speaking in slow, soft tones. "Poor Chauvet's death was sudden, but from his written instructions I fancy he was not unprepared. He has no relatives,—and he must have found great consolation in making his will in your favour. For he cared very greatly for you,—he told me he had asked you to marry him."

Diana moved a little restlessly. As she did so a rosy flash glittered from a great jewel she wore round her neck,— the famous "Eye of Rajuna," whose tragic history she had heard from Chauvet himself.

"Yes," she answered—"That is true. But—I forgot!"

"You forgot?" he echoed, wonderingly. "You forgot a proposal of marriage? And yet—when you came to me first in Geneva you thought love was enough for everything,— your heart was hungry for love——"

"When I had a heart—yes!" she said. "But now I have none. And I do not hunger for what does not exist! I am sorry I forgot the kind Professor. But I did,—completely! And that he should have left me all he possessed is almost a punishment!"

"You should not regard it as such," he answered. "It is hardly your fault if you forgot. Your thoughts are, perhaps, elsewhere?" He paused,—but she said nothing. "As I have told you," he went on, "Chauvet has left you an ample fortune, together with this house and all it contains—its unique library, its pictures and curios, to say nothing of his famous collection of jewels, worth many thousands of pounds—and as everything is in perfect order you will have no trouble. Personally, I had no idea he was such a wealthy man."

She was still silent, looking at him more or less critically. He felt her eyes upon him, and some impulse stung him into sudden fervour.

"You look indifferent," he said, "and no doubt you *are* indifferent. Your nature now admits of no emotion. But, so far as you are woman, your circumstances are little changed. You are as you were when you first became my 'subject'—'of mature years, and alone in the world without claims on your time or your affections.' Is it not so?"

A faint, mysterious smile lifted the corners of her lovely mouth.

"It is so!" she answered.

"You are alone in the world,—alone, alone, alone!" he repeated with a kind of fierce intensity. "Alone!—for I know that neither your father nor your mother recognise you. Am I right or wrong?"

Still smiling, she bent her head.

"Right, of course!" she murmured, with delicate irony. "How could *you* be wrong!"

"Your own familiar friends will have none of you," he went on, with almost angry emphasis. "To the world you once knew, you are dead! The man who was your lover—the man who, as you told me, spoilt your life and on whom you seek to be revenged——"

She lifted one hand with an interrupting gesture.

"That is finished," she said. "I seek vengeance no longer. No man is worth it! Besides, I *am* avenged."

She half rose from her reclining attitude, and he waited for her next word.

"I am avenged!" she went on, in thrilling accents—"And in a way that satisfies me. My lover that was,—never a true lover at best,—is my lover still—but with such limitations as are torture to a man whose only sense of love is—Desire! My beauty fills him with longing,—the thought of me ravages his soul and body—it occupies every thought and every dream!—and with this passion comes the consciousness of age. Age!—the great breakdown!—the end of all for *him*!—I have willed that he shall feel its numbing approach each day,—that he shall know the time is near when his step shall fail, his sight grow dim,—when the rush of youthful life shall pass him by and leave him desolate. Yes!—I am avenged!—he is 'old enough now to realise that we are better apart!'"

Her eyes glowed like stars,—her whole face was radiant. Dimitrius gazed at her almost sternly.

"You are pitiless!" he said.

She laughed.

"As *he* was,—yes!" And rising to her full height, she stood up like a queen. She wore a robe of dull amber stuff interwoven with threads of gold,—a small circlet of diamonds glittered in her hair, and Chauvet's historic Eastern jewel, the "Eye of Rajuna," flamed like fire on her white neck.

"Féodor Dimitrius," she said,—and her voice had such a marvellously sweet intonation that he felt it penetrate through every nerve—"You say, and you say rightly, that 'so far as I am woman'—my circumstances are not changed from what they were when I first came to you in Geneva. But only 'so far as I am woman.' Now—how do you know I am woman at all?"

He lifted himself in his chair, gripping both arms of it with clenched nervous hands. His dark eyes flashed a piercing inquiry into hers.

"What do you mean?" he half whispered. "What—what would you make me believe?"

She smiled. "Oh, marvellous man of science!" she exclaimed—"Must I teach you your own discovery? You, who have studied and mastered the fusion of light and air with elemental forces and the invisible whirl of electrons with perpetually changing forms, must I, your subject, explain to you what you have done? You have wrested a marvellous secret from Nature—you can unmake and remake the human body, freeing it from all gross substance, as a sculptor can mould and unmould a statue,—and do you not see that you have made of me a new creature, no longer of mere mortal clay, but of an ethereal matter which has never walked on earth before?—and with which earth has nothing in common? What have such as I to do with such base trifles as human vengeance or love?"

He sprang up and approached her.

"Diana," he said slowly—"If this is true,—and may God be the arbiter!—one thing in your former circumstances is altered—you are not 'without claims on your time and your affections.' *I* claim both! I have made you as you are!—you are mine!"

She smiled proudly and retreated a step or two.

"I am no more yours," she said, "than are the elements of which your science has composed the new and youthful vesture of my unchanging Soul! I admit no claim. When I served you as your 'subject,' you were ready to sacrifice my life to your ambition; now when you are witness to the triumph of your 'experiment,' you would grasp what you consider as your lawful prize. Self!—all Self! But I have a Self as well—and it is a Self independent of all save its own elements."

He caught her hands suddenly.

"Love is in all elements," he said. "There would be no world, no universe without love!"

Her eyes met his as steadily as stars.

"There is no such thing as Love in all mankind!" she said. "The race is cruel, destructive, murderous. What men call love is merely sex-attraction—such as is common to all the animal world. Children are to be born in order that man may be perpetuated. *Why*, one cannot imagine! His civilisations perish—he himself is the merest grain of dust in the universe,—unless he learns to subdue his passions and progresses to a higher order of being on this earth, which he never will. All things truly are possible, save man's own voluntary uplifting. And without this uplifting there is no such thing as Love."

He still held her hands.

"May I not endeavour to reach this height?" he asked, and his voice shook a little. "Have patience with me, Diana! You have beauty, wealth, youth——"

She interrupted him.

"You forget! 'Mature years' are in my brain and heart,—I am not really young."

"You *are*," he rejoined—"Younger than you can as yet realise. You see your own outward appearance, but you have had no time yet to test your inward emotions——"

"I have none!" she said.

He dropped her hands. "Not even an angel's attribute —mercy?"

A faint sigh stirred her bosom where the great "Eye of Rajuna" shone like a red star.

"Perhaps!——" she said—"I do not know—it may be possible!"

1917–1918

7 YVA

H. Rider Haggard

Marooned on a South Sea island, Humphrey Arbuthnot and his companions, the skeptical Bickley and the devout Bastin, discover two superhuman survivors of an ancient, technologically advanced race who've spent 250,000 years entombed (in the underground city of Nyo) in a state of suspended animation. The tyrannical Lord Oro is concerned to learn whether he ought once again to destroy the planet by flooding . . . and whether there is any truth to the newfangled Christian notion of life after death. His daughter Yva, meanwhile, is a more sympathetic figure.

* * *

On the following morning we despatched Bastin to keep his rendezvous in the sepulchre at the proper time. Had we not done so I felt sure that he would have forgotten it, for on this occasion he was for once an unwilling missioner. He tried to persuade one of us to come with him—even Bickley would have been welcome; but we both declared that we could not dream of interfering in such a professional matter; also that our presence was forbidden, and would certainly distract the attention of his pupil.

"What you mean," said the gloomy Bastin, "is that you intend to enjoy yourselves up here in the female companionship of the Glittering Lady whilst I sit thousands of feet underground attempting to lighten the darkness of a violent old sinner whom I suspect of being in league with Satan."

"With whom you should be proud to break a lance," said Bickley.

"So I am, in the daylight. For instance, when he uses *your* mouth to advance his arguments, Bickley, but this is another matter. However, if I do not appear again you will know that I died in a good cause, and, I hope, try to recover my remains and give them decent burial. Also, you might inform the Bishop of how I came to my end, that is, if you ever get an opportunity, which is more than doubtful."

"Hurry up, Bastin, hurry up!" said the unfeeling Bickley, "or you will be late for your appointment and put your would-be neophyte into a bad temper."

Then Bastin went, carrying under his arm a large Bible printed in the language of the South Sea Islands.

A little while later Yva appeared, arrayed in her wondrous robes which, being a man, it is quite impossible for me to describe. She saw us looking at these, and, after greeting us both, also [my spaniel] Tommy, who was enraptured at her coming, asked us how the ladies of our country attired themselves.

We tried to explain, with no striking success.

"You are as stupid about such matters as were the men of the Old World," she said, shaking her head and laughing. "I thought that you had with you pictures of ladies you have known which would show me."

Now, in fact, I had in a pocket-book a photograph of my wife in evening-dress, also a miniature of her head and bust painted on ivory, a beautiful piece of work done by a master hand, which I always wore. These, after a moment's hesitation, I produced and showed to her, Bickley having gone away for a little while to see about something connected with his attempted analysis of the Life-water. She examined them with great eagerness, and as she did so I noted that her face grew tender and troubled.

"This was your wife," she said as one who states what she knows to be a fact. I nodded, and she went on: "She was sweet and beautiful as a flower, but not so tall as I am, I think."

"No," I answered, "she lacked height; given that she would have been a lovely woman."

"I am glad you think that women should be tall," she said, glancing at her shadow. "The eyes were such as mine, were they not—in colour, I mean?"

"Yes, very like yours, only yours are larger."

"That is a beautiful way of wearing the hair. Would you be angry if I tried it? I weary of this old fashion."

"Why should I be angry?" I asked.

At this moment Bickley reappeared and she began to talk of the details of the dress, saying that it showed more of the neck than had been the custom among the women of her people, but was very pretty.

"That is because we are still barbarians," said Bickley; "at least, our women are, and therefore rely upon primitive methods of attraction, like the savages yonder."

She smiled, and, after a last, long glance, gave me back the photograph and the miniature, saying as she delivered the latter: "I rejoice to see that you are faithful, Humphrey, and wear this picture on your heart, as well as in it."

"Then you must be a very remarkable woman," said Bickley. "Never before did I hear one of your sex rejoice because a man was faithful to somebody else."

"Has Bickley been disappointed in his love-heart, that he is so angry with us women?" asked Yva innocently of me. Then, without waiting for an answer, she inquired of him whether he had been successful in his analysis of the Life-water.

"How do you know what I was doing with the Life-water? Did Bastin tell you?" exclaimed Bickley.

"Bastin told me nothing, except that he was afraid of the descent to Nyo; that he hated Nyo when he reached it, as indeed I do, and that he thought that my father, the Lord Oro, was a devil or evil spirit from some Under-world which he called hell."

"Bastin has an open heart and an open mouth," said Bickley, "for which I respect him. Follow his example if you will, Lady Yva, and tell us who and what is the Lord Oro, and who and what are you."

"Have we not done so already? If not, I will repeat. The Lord Oro and I are two who have lived on from the old time when the world was different, and yet, I think, the same. He is a man and not a god, and I am a woman. His powers are great because of his knowledge, which he has gathered from his forefathers and in a life of a thousand years before he went to sleep. He can do things you cannot do. Thus, he can pass through space and take others with him, and return again. He can learn what is happening in far-off parts of the world, as he did when he told you of the war in which your country is concerned. He has terrible powers; for instance, he can kill, as he killed those savages. Also, he knows the secrets of the earth, and, if it pleases him, can change its turning so that earthquakes happen and sea becomes land, and land sea, and the places that were hot grow cold, and those that were cold grow hot."

"All of which things have happened many times in the history of the globe," said Bickley, "without the help of the Lord Oro."

"Others had knowledge before my father, and others doubtless will have knowledge after him. Even I, Yva, have some knowledge, and knowledge is strength."

"Yes," I interposed, "but such powers as you attribute to your father are not given to man."

"You mean to man as you know him, man like Bickley, who thinks that he has learned everything that was ever learned. But it is not so. Hundreds of thousands of years ago men knew more than it seems they do today, ten times more, as they lived ten times longer, or so you tell me."

"Men?" I said.

"Yes, men, not gods or spirits, as the uninstructed nations supposed them to be. My father is a man subject to the hopes and terrors of man. He desires power which is ambition, and when the world refused his rule, he destroyed that part of it which rebelled, which is revenge.

Moreover, above all things he dreads death, which is fear. That is why he suspended life in himself and me for two hundred and fifty thousand years, as his knowledge gave him strength to do, because death was near and he thought that sleep was better than death."

"Why should he dread to die," asked Bickley, "seeing that sleep and death are the same?"

"Because his knowledge tells him that Sleep and Death are *not* the same, as you, in your foolishness, believe, for there Bastin is wiser than you. Because for all his wisdom he remains ignorant of what happens to man when the Light of Life is blown out by the breath of Fate. That is why he fears to die and why he talks with Bastin the Preacher, who says he has the secret of the future."

"And do you fear to die?" I asked.

"No, Humphrey," she answered gently. "Because I think that there is no death, and, having done no wrong, I dread no evil. I had dreams while I was asleep, O Humphrey, and it seemed to me that—"

Here she ceased and glanced at where she knew the miniature was hanging upon my breast.

"Now," she continued, after a little pause, "tell me of your world, of its history, of its languages, of what happens there, for I long to know."

So then and there, assisted by Bickley, I began the education of the Lady Yva. I do not suppose that there was ever a more apt pupil in the whole earth. To begin with, she was better acquainted with every subject on which I touched than I was myself; all she lacked was information as to its modern aspect. Her knowledge ended two hundred and fifty thousand years ago, at which date, however, it would seem that civilisation had already touched a higher water-mark than it has ever since attained. Thus, this vanished people understood astronomy, natural magnetism, the force of gravity, steam, also electricity to some subtle use of which, I gathered, the lighting of their underground city was to be attributed. They had mastered architecture and the arts, as their buildings and statues showed; they could fly through the air better than we have learned to do within the last few years.

More, they, or some of them, had learned the use of the Fourth Dimension, that is their most instructed individuals, could move *through* opposing things, as well as over them, up into them and across them. This power these possessed in a two-fold form. I mean, that they could either disintegrate their bodies at one spot and cause them to integrate again at another, or they could project what the old Egyptians called the Ka or Double, and modern Theosophists name the Astral Shape, to any distance. Moreover, this Double, or Astral Shape, while itself invisible, still, so to speak, had the use of its senses. It could see, it could hear, and it could remember, and, on returning to the body, it could avail itself of the experience thus acquired.

Thus, at least, said Yva, while Bickley contemplated her with a cold and unbelieving eye. She even went further and alleged that in certain instances, individuals of her extinct race had been able to pass through the ether and to visit other worlds in the depths of space.

"Have you ever done that?" asked Bickley.

"Once or twice I dreamed that I did," she replied quietly.

"We can all dream," he answered.

As it was my lot to make acquaintance with this strange and uncanny power at a later date, I will say no more of it now.

Telepathy, she declared, was also a developed gift among the Sons of Wisdom; indeed, they seem to have used it as we use wireless messages. Only, in their case, the sending and receiving stations were skilled and susceptible human beings who went on duty for so many hours at a time. Thus intelligence was transmitted with accuracy and despatch. Those who had this faculty were, she said, also very apt at reading the minds of others and therefore not easy to deceive.

"Is that how you know that I had been trying to analyse your Life-water?" asked Bickley.

"Yes," she answered, with her unvarying smile. "At the moment I spoke thereof you were wondering whether my father would be angry if he knew that you had taken the water in a little flask." She studied him for a moment, then added: "Now you are wondering, first, whether I did not see you take the water from the fountain and guess the purpose, and, secondly, whether perhaps Bastin did not tell me what you were doing with it when we met in the sepulchre."

"Look here," said the exasperated Bickley, "I admit that telepathy and thought-reading are possible to a certain limited extent. But supposing that you possess those powers, as I think in English, and you do not know English, how can you interpret what is passing in my mind?"

"Perhaps you have been teaching me English all this while without knowing it, Bickley. In any case, it matters little, seeing that what I read is the thought, not the language with which it is clothed. The thought comes from your mind to mine—that is, if I wish it, which is not often—and I interpret it in my own or other tongues."

"I am glad to hear it is not often, Lady Yva, since thoughts are generally considered private."

"Yes, and therefore I will read yours no more. Why should I, when they are so full of disbelief of all I tell you, and sometimes of other things about myself which I do not seek to know?"

"No wonder that, according to the story in the pictures, those Nations, whom you named Barbarians, made an end of your people, Lady Yva."

"You are mistaken, Bickley; the Lord Oro made an end of the Nations, though against my prayer," she added with a sigh.

Then Bickley departed in a rage, and did not appear again for an hour.

"He is angry," she said, looking after him; "nor do I wonder. It is hard for the very clever like Bickley, who think that they have mastered all things, to find that after all they are quite ignorant. I am sorry for him, and I like him very much."

"Then you would be sorry for me also, Lady Yva?"

"Why?" she asked with a dazzling smile, "when your heart is athirst for knowledge, gaping for it like a fledgling's mouth for food, and, as it chances, though I am not very wise, I can satisfy something of your soul-hunger."

"Not very wise!" I repeated.

"No, Humphrey. I think that Bastin, who in many ways is so stupid, has more true wisdom than I have, because he can believe and accept without question. After all, the wisdom of my people is all of the universe and its wonders. What you think magic is not magic; it is only gathered knowledge and the finding out of secrets. Bickley will tell you the same, although as yet he does not believe that the mind of man can stretch so far."

"You mean that your wisdom has in it nothing of the spirit?"

"Yes, Humphrey, that is what I mean. I do not even know if there is such a thing as spirit. Our god was Fate; Bastin's god is a spirit, and I think yours also."

"Yes."

"Therefore, I wish you and Bastin to teach me of your god, as does Oro, my father. I want—oh! so much, Humphrey, to learn whether we live after death."

"You!" I exclaimed. "You who, according to the story, have slept for two hundred and fifty thousand years! You, who have, unless I mistake, hinted that during that sleep you may have lived in other shapes! Do you doubt whether we can live after death?"

"Yes. Sleep induced by secret arts is not death, and during that sleep the *I* within might wander and inhabit other shapes, because it is forbidden to be idle. Moreover, what seems to be death may not be death, only another form of sleep from which the *I* awakes again upon the world. But at last comes the real death, when the *I* is extinguished to the world. That much I know, because my people learned it."

"You mean, you know that men and women may live again and again upon the world?"

"Yes, Humphrey, I do. For in the world there is only a certain store of life which in many forms travels on and on, till the lot of each *I* is fulfilled. Then comes the real death, and after that—what, oh!—what?"

"You must ask Bastin," I said humbly. "I cannot dare to teach of such matters."

1919

8 ZOO

George Bernard Shaw

In the early twentieth century, according to "Tragedy of an Elderly Gentleman: A.D. 3000," one of five plays within Shaw's "metabiological Pentateuch" *Back to Methuselah*, the secret of Creative Evolution (i.e., the process by which an organism can will its own *entelechy*, or self-potentiation) is discovered. A millennium or so later, we meet Zoo, a longlived superwoman who has been assigned the task of "nursing" short-lived pilgrims seeking oracular advice, lest they should fatally succumb to discouragement. In the following excerpt, Zoo tries in vain to communicate with a non-superhuman "shortliver" on a pilgrimage to her colony from British Baghdad.

* * *

THE ELDERLY GENTLEMAN. [*after looking cautiously round*] I do not approve of microscopes. I never have.

ZOO. You call that advanced! Oh, Daddy, that is pure obscurantism.

THE ELDERLY GENTLEMAN. Call it so if you will, madam; but I maintain that it is dangerous to shew too much to people who do not know what they are looking at. I think that a man who is sane as long as he looks at the world through his own eyes is very likely to become a dangerous madman if he takes to looking at the world through telescopes and microscopes. Even when he is telling fairy stories about giants and dwarfs, the giants had better not be too big nor the dwarfs too small and too malicious. Before the microscope came, our fairy stories only made the children's flesh creep pleasantly, and did not frighten grown-up persons at all. But the microscope men terrified themselves and everyone else out of their wits with the invisible monsters they saw: poor harmless little things that die at the touch of a ray of sunshine, and are themselves the victims of all the diseases they are supposed to produce! Whatever the scientific people may say, imagination without microscopes was kindly and often courageous, because it worked on things of which it had some real knowledge. But imagination with microscopes, working on a terrifying spectacle of millions of grotesque creatures of whose nature it had no knowledge, became a cruel, terror-stricken, persecuting delirium. Are you aware, madam, that a general massacre of men of science took place in the twenty-first century of the pseudo-Christian era, when all their laboratories were demolished, and all their apparatus destroyed?

ZOO. Yes: the shortlived are as savage in their advances as in their relapses. But when Science crept back, it had been taught its place. The mere collectors of anatomical or chemical facts were not supposed to know more about Science than the collector of used postage stamps about international trade or literature. The scientific terrorist who was afraid to use a spoon or a tumbler until he had dipt it in some poisonous acid to kill the microbes, was no longer given titles, pensions, and monstrous powers over the bodies of other people: he was sent to an asylum, and treated there until his recovery. But all that is an old story: the extension of life to three hundred years has provided the human race with capable leaders, and made short work of such childish stuff.

THE ELDERLY GENTLEMAN. [*pettishly*] You seem to credit every advance in civilization to your inordinately long lives. Do you not know that this question was familiar to men who died before they had reached my own age?

ZOO. Oh yes: one or two of them hinted at it in a feeble way. An ancient writer whose name has come down to us in several forms, such as Shakespear, Shelley, Sheridan, and Shoddy, has a remarkable passage about your dispositions being horridly shaken by thoughts beyond the reaches of your souls. That does not come to much, does it?

THE ELDERLY GENTLEMAN. At all events, madam, I may remind you, if you come to capping ages, that whatever your secondaries and tertiaries may be, you are younger than I am.

ZOO. Yes, Daddy; but it is not the number of years we have behind us, but the number we have before us, that makes us careful and responsible and determined to find out the truth about everything. What does it matter to you whether anything is true or not? your flesh is as grass: you come up like a flower, and wither in your second childhood. A lie will last your time: it will not last mine. If I knew I had to die in twenty years it would not be worth my while to educate myself: I should not bother about anything but having a little pleasure while I lasted.

THE ELDERLY GENTLEMAN. Young woman: you are mistaken. Shortlived as we are, we—the best of us, I mean—

regard civilization and learning, art and science, as an ever-burning torch, which passes from the hand of one generation to the hand of the next, each generation kindling it to a brighter, prouder flame. Thus each lifetime, however short, contributes a brick to a vast and growing edifice, a page to a sacred volume, a chapter to a Bible, a Bible to a literature. We may be insects; but like the coral insect we build islands which become continents: like the bee we store sustenance for future communities. The individual perishes; but the race is immortal. The acorn of today is the oak of the next millennium. I throw my stone on the cairn and die; but later comers add another stone and yet another; and lo! a mountain. I—

ZOO. [*interrupts him by laughing heartily at him*] !!!!!!

THE ELDERLY GENTLEMAN. [*with offended dignity*] May I ask what I have said that calls for this merriment?

ZOO. Oh, Daddy, Daddy, Daddy, you are a funny little man, with your torches, and your flames, and your bricks and edifices and pages and volumes and chapters and coral insects and bees and acorns and stones and mountains.

THE ELDERLY GENTLEMAN. Metaphors, madam. Metaphors merely.

ZOO. Images, images, images. I was talking about men, not about images.

THE ELDERLY GENTLEMAN. I was illustrating—not, I hope, quite infelicitously—the great march of Progress. I was shewing you how, shortlived as we orientals are, mankind gains in stature from generation to generation, from epoch to epoch, from barbarism to civilization, from civilization to perfection.

ZOO. I see. The father grows to be six feet high, and hands on his six feet to his son, who adds another six feet and becomes twelve feet high, and hands his twelve feet on to his son, who is full-grown at eighteen feet, and so on. In a thousand years you would all be three or four miles high. At that rate your ancestors Bilge and Bluebeard, whom you call giants, must have been about quarter of an inch high.

THE ELDERLY GENTLEMAN. I am not here to bandy quibbles and paradoxes with a girl who blunders over the greatest names in history. I am in earnest. I am treating a solemn theme seriously. I never said that the son of a man six feet high would be twelve feet high.

ZOO. You didn't mean that?

THE ELDERLY GENTLEMAN. Most certainly not.

ZOO. Then you didn't mean anything. Now listen to me, you little ephemeral thing. I knew quite well what you meant by your torch handed on from generation to generation. But every time that torch is handed on, it dies down to the tiniest spark; and the man who gets it can rekindle it only by his own light. You are no taller than Bilge or Bluebeard; and you are no wiser. Their wisdom, such as it was, perished with them: so did their strength, if their strength ever existed outside your imagination. I do not know how old you are: you look about five hundred—

THE ELDERLY GENTLEMAN. Five hundred! Really, madam—

ZOO. [*continuing*]; but I know, of course, that you are an ordinary shortliver. Well, your wisdom is only such wisdom as a man can have before he has had experience enough to distinguish his wisdom from his folly, his destiny from his delusions, his—

THE ELDERLY GENTLEMAN. In short, such wisdom as your own.

ZOO. No, no, no, no. How often must I tell you that we are made wise not by the recollections of our past, but by the responsibilities of our future. I shall be more reckless when I am a tertiary than I am today. If you cannot understand that, at least you must admit that I have learnt from tertiaries. I have seen their work and lived under their institutions. Like all young things I rebelled against them; and in their hunger for new lights and new ideas they listened to me and encouraged me to rebel. But my ways did not work; and theirs did; and they were able to tell me why. They have no power over me except that power: they refuse all other power; and the consequence is that there are no limits to their power except the limits they set themselves. You are a child governed by children, who make so many mistakes and are so naughty that you are in continual rebellion against them; and as they can never convince you that they are right: they can govern you only by beating you, imprisoning you, torturing you, killing you if you disobey them without being strong enough to kill or torture them.

THE ELDERLY GENTLEMAN. That may be an unfortunate fact. I condemn it and deplore it. But our minds are greater than the facts. We know better. The greatest ancient teachers, followed by the galaxy of Christs who arose in the twentieth century, not to mention such comparatively modern spiritual leaders as Blitherinjam, Tosh, and Spiffkins, all taught that punishment and revenge, coercion and militarism, are mistakes, and that the golden rule—

ZOO. [*interrupting*] Yes, yes, yes, Daddy: we longlived people know that quite well. But did any of their disciples ever succeed in governing you for a single day on their Christlike principles? It is not enough to know what is good: you must be able to do it. They couldn't do it because they did not live long enough to find out how to do it, or to outlive the childish passions that prevented them from really wanting to do it. You know very well that they could only keep order—such as it was—by the very coercion and militarism they were denouncing and deploring. They had actually to kill one another for preaching their own gospel, or be killed themselves.

THE ELDERLY GENTLEMAN. The blood of the martyrs, madam, is the seed of the Church.

ZOO. More images, Daddy! The blood of the shortlived falls on stony ground.

THE ELDERLY GENTLEMAN. [*rising, very testy*] You are simply mad on the subject of longevity. I wish you would change it. It is rather personal and in bad taste. Human nature is human nature, longlived or shortlived, and always will be.

ZOO. Then you give up the idea of progress? You cry off the torch, and the brick, and the acorn, and all the rest of it?

THE ELDERLY GENTLEMAN. I do nothing of the sort. I stand for progress and for freedom broadening down from precedent to precedent.

ZOO. You are certainly a true Briton.

THE ELDERLY GENTLEMAN. I am proud of it. But in your mouth I feel that the compliment hides some insult; so I do not thank you for it.

ZOO. All I meant was that though Britons sometimes say quite clever things and deep things as well as silly and shallow things, they always forget them ten minutes after they have uttered them.

THE ELDERLY GENTLEMAN. Leave it at that, madam: leave it at that. [*He sits down again*]. Even a Pope is not expected to be continually pontificating. Our flashes of inspiration shew that our hearts are in the right place.

ZOO. Of course. You cannot keep your heart in any place but the right place.

THE ELDERLY GENTLEMAN. Tcha!

ZOO. But you can keep your hands in the wrong place. In your neighbor's pockets, for example. So, you see, it is your hands that really matter.

THE ELDERLY GENTLEMAN. [*exhausted*] Well, a woman must have the last word. I will not dispute it with you.

ZOO. Good. Now let us go back to the really interesting subject of our discussion. You remember? The slavery of the shortlived to images and metaphors.

THE ELDERLY GENTLEMAN. [*aghast*] Do you mean to say, madam, that after having talked my head off, and reduced me to despair and silence by your intolerable loquacity, you actually propose to begin all over again? I shall leave you at once.

ZOO. You must not. I am your nurse; and you must stay with me.

THE ELDERLY GENTLEMAN. I absolutely decline to do anything of the sort [*he rises and walks away with marked dignity*].

ZOO. [*using her tuning-fork*] Zoo on Burrin Pier to Oracle Police at Ennistymon have you got me? ... What? ... I am picking you up now but you are flat to my pitch. ... Just a shade sharper. ... That's better: still a little more. ... Got you: right. Isolate Burrin Pier quick.

THE ELDERLY GENTLEMAN. [*is heard to yell*] Oh!

ZOO. [*still intoning*] Thanks. ... Oh nothing serious ... I am nursing a shortliver and the silly creature has run away ... He has discouraged himself very badly by gadding about and talking to secondaries and I must keep him strictly to heel.

The Elderly Gentleman returns, indignant.

ZOO. Here he is—you can release the Pier thanks. Goodbye. [*She puts up her tuning-fork*].

THE ELDERLY GENTLEMAN. This is outrageous. When I tried to step off the pier onto the road, I received a shock, followed by an attack of pins and needles which ceased only when I stepped back on to the stones.

ZOO. Yes: there is an electric hedge there. It is a very old and very crude method of keeping animals from straying.

THE ELDERLY GENTLEMAN. We are perfectly familiar with it in Baghdad, madam; but I little thought I should live to have it ignominiously applied to myself. You have actually Kiplingized me.

ZOO. Kiplingized! What is that?

THE ELDERLY GENTLEMAN. About a thousand years ago there were two authors named Kipling. One was an eastern and a writer of merit: the other, being a western, was of course only an amusing barbarian. He is said to have invented the electric hedge. I consider that in using it on me you have taken a very great liberty.

ZOO. What is a liberty?

THE ELDERLY GENTLEMAN. [*exasperated*] I shall not explain, madam. I believe you know as well as I do. [*He sits down on the bollard in dudgeon*].

ZOO. No: even you can tell me things I do not know. Haven't you noticed that all the time you have been here we have been asking you questions?

THE ELDERLY GENTLEMAN. Noticed it! It has almost driven me mad. Do you see my white hair? It was hardly grey when I landed: there were patches of its original auburn still distinctly discernible.

ZOO. That is one of the symptoms of discouragement. But have you noticed something much more important to yourself: that is, that you have never asked us any questions, although we know so much more than you do?

THE ELDERLY GENTLEMAN. I am not a child, madam. I believe I have had occasion to say that before. And I am an experienced traveller. I know that what the traveller observes must really exist, or he could not observe it. But what the natives tell him is invariably pure fiction.

ZOO. Not here, Daddy. With us life is too long for telling lies. They all get found out. You'd better ask me questions while you have the chance.

THE ELDERLY GENTLEMAN. If I have occasion to consult the oracle I shall address myself to a proper one: to a tertiary: not to a primary flapper playing at being an oracle. If you are a nursery maid, attend to your duties; and do not presume to ape your elders.

ZOO. [*rising ominously and reddening*] You silly—

THE ELDERLY GENTLEMAN. [*thundering*] Silence! Do you hear? Hold your tongue.

ZOO. Something very disagreeable is happening to me. I feel hot all over. I have a horrible impulse to injure you. What have you done to me?

THE ELDERLY GENTLEMAN. [*triumphant*] Aha! I have made you blush. Now you know what blushing means. Blushing with shame!

ZOO. Whatever you are doing, it is something so utterly evil that if you do not stop I will kill you.

THE ELDERLY GENTLEMAN. [*apprehending his danger*] Doubtless you think it safe to threaten an old man—

ZOO. [*fiercely*] Old! You are a child: an evil child. We kill evil children here. We do it even against our own wills by instinct. Take care.

THE ELDERLY GENTLEMAN. [*rising with crestfallen courtesy*] I did not mean to hurt your feelings. I—[*swallowing the apology with an effort*] I beg your pardon. [*He takes off his hat, and bows*].

ZOO. What does that mean?

THE ELDERLY GENTLEMAN. I withdraw what I said.

ZOO. How can you withdraw what you said?

THE ELDERLY GENTLEMAN. I can say no more than that I am sorry.

ZOO. You have reason to be. That hideous sensation you gave me is subsiding; but you have had a very narrow escape. Do not attempt to kill me again; for at the first sign in your voice or face I shall strike you dead.

THE ELDERLY GENTLEMAN. *I* attempt to kill you! What a monstrous accusation!

ZOO. [*frowns*]!

THE ELDERLY GENTLEMAN. [*prudently correcting himself*] I mean misunderstanding. I never dreamt of such a thing. Surely you cannot believe that I am a murderer.

ZOO. I know you are a murderer. It is not merely that you threw words at me as if they were stones, meaning to hurt me. It was the instinct to kill that you roused in me. I did not know it was in my nature: never before has it wakened and sprung out at me, warning me to kill or be killed. I must now reconsider my whole political position. I am no longer a Conservative.

THE ELDERLY GENTLEMAN. [*dropping his hat*] Gracious Heavens! you have lost your senses. I am at the mercy of a madwoman: I might have known it from the beginning. I can bear no more of this. [*Offering his chest for the sacrifice*] Kill me at once; and much good may my death do you!

ZOO. It would be useless unless all the other shortlivers were killed at the same time. Besides, it is a measure which should be taken politically and constitutionally, not privately. However, I am prepared to discuss it with you.

THE ELDERLY GENTLEMAN. No, no, no. I had much rather discuss your intention of withdrawing from the Conservative party. How the Conservatives have tolerated your opinions so far is more than I can imagine: I can only conjecture that you have contributed very liberally to the party funds. [*He picks up his hat, and sits down again*].

ZOO. Do not babble so senselessly: our chief political controversy is the most momentous in the world for you and your like.

THE ELDERLY GENTLEMAN. [*interested*] Indeed? Pray, may I ask what it is? I am a keen politician, and may perhaps be of some use. [*He puts on his hat, cocking it slightly*].

ZOO. We have two great parties: the Conservative party and the Colonization party. The Colonizers are of the opinion that we should increase our numbers and colonize. The Conservatives hold that we should stay as we are, confined to these islands, a race apart, wrapped up in the majesty of our wisdom on a soil held as holy ground for us by an adoring world, with our sacred frontier traced beyond dispute by the sea. They contend that it is our destiny to rule the world, and that even when we were shortlived we did so. They say that our power and our peace depend on our remoteness, our exclusiveness, our separation, and the restriction of our numbers. Five minutes ago that was my political faith. Now I do not think there should be any shortlived people at all. [*She throws herself again carelessly on the sacks*].

THE ELDERLY GENTLEMAN. Am I to infer that you deny my right to live because I allowed myself—perhaps injudiciously—to give you a slight scolding?

ZOO. Is it worth living for so short a time? Are you any good to yourself?

THE ELDERLY GENTLEMAN. [*stupent*] Well, upon my soul!

ZOO. It is such a very little soul. You only encourage the sin of pride in us, and keep us looking down at you instead of up to something higher than ourselves.

THE ELDERLY GENTLEMAN. Is not that a selfish view, madam? Think of the good you do us by your oracular counsels!

ZOO. What good have our counsels ever done you? You come to us for advice when you know you are in difficulties. But you never know you are in difficulties until twenty years after you have made the mistakes that led to them; and then it is too late. You cannot understand our advice: you often do more mischief by trying to act on it than if you had been left to your own childish devices. If you were not childish you would not come to us at all: you would learn from experience that your consultations of the oracle are never of any real help to you. You draw wonderful imaginary pictures of us, and write fictitious tales and poems about our beneficent operations in the past, our wisdom, our justice, our mercy: stories in which we often appear as sentimental dupes of your prayers and sacrifices; but you do it only to conceal from yourselves the truth that you are incapable of being helped by us. Your Prime Minister pretends that he has come to be guided by the oracle; but we are not deceived: we know quite well that he has come here so that when he goes back he may have the authority and dignity of one who has visited the holy islands and spoken face to face with the ineffable ones. He will pretend that all the measures he wishes to take for his own purposes have been enjoined on him by the oracle.

THE ELDERLY GENTLEMAN. But you forget that the answers of the oracle cannot be kept secret or misrepresented. They are written and promulgated. The Leader of the Opposition can obtain copies. All the nations know them. Secret diplomacy has been totally abolished.

ZOO. Yes: you publish documents; but they are garbled or forged. And even if you published our real answers it would make no difference, because the shortlived cannot interpret the plainest writings. Your scriptures command you in the plainest terms to do exactly the contrary of everything your own laws and chosen rulers command and execute. You cannot defy Nature. It is a law of Nature that there is a fixed relation between conduct and length of life.

THE ELDERLY GENTLEMAN. I have never heard of any such law, madam.

ZOO. Well, you are hearing of it now.

THE ELDERLY GENTLEMAN. Let me tell you that we shortlivers, as you call us, have lengthened our lives very considerably.

ZOO. How?

THE ELDERLY GENTLEMAN. By saving time. By enabling men to cross the ocean in an afternoon, and to see and speak to one another when they are thousands of miles apart. We hope shortly to organize their labor, and press natural forces into their service, so scientifically that the burden of labor will cease to be perceptible, leaving common men more leisure than they will know what to do with.

ZOO. Daddy: the man whose life is lengthened in this way may be busier than a savage; but the difference between such men living seventy years and those living three hundred would be all the greater; for to a shortliver increase of years is only increase of sorrow; but to a longliver every extra year is a prospect which forces him to stretch his faculties to the utmost to face it. Therefore I say that we who live three hundred years can be of no use to you who live less than a hundred, and that our true destiny is not to advise and govern you, but to supplant and supersede you. In that faith I now declare myself a Colonizer and an Exterminator.

THE ELDERLY GENTLEMAN. Oh, steady! steady! Pray! pray! Reflect, I implore you. It is possible to colonize without exterminating the natives. Would you treat us less mercifully than our barbarous forefathers treated the Redskin and the Negro? Are we not, as Britons, entitled at least to some reservations?

ZOO. What is the use of prolonging the agony? You would perish slowly in our presence, no matter what we did to preserve you. You were almost dead when I took charge of you today, merely because you had talked for a few minutes to a secondary. Besides, we have our own experience to go upon. Have you never heard that our children occasionally revert to the ancestral type, and are born shortlived?

THE ELDERLY GENTLEMAN. [*eagerly*] Never. I hope you will not be offended if I say that it would be a great comfort to me if I could be placed in charge of one of those normal individuals.

ZOO. Abnormal, you mean. What you ask is impossible: we weed them all out.

THE ELDERLY GENTLEMAN. When you say that you weed them out, you send a cold shiver down my spine. I hope you don't mean that you—that you—that you assist Nature in any way?

ZOO. Why not? Have you not heard the saying of the Chinese sage Dee Ning, that a good garden needs weeding? But it is not necessary for us to interfere. We are naturally rather particular as to the conditions on which we consent to live. One does not mind the accidental loss of an arm or a leg or an eye: after all, no one with two legs is unhappy because he has not three; so why should a man with one be unhappy because he has not two? But infirmities of mind and temper are quite another matter. If one of us has no self-control, or is too weak to bear the strain of our truthful life without wincing, or is tormented by depraved appetites and superstitions, or is unable to keep free from pain and depression, he naturally becomes discouraged, and refuses to live.

THE ELDERLY GENTLEMAN. Good Lord! Cuts his throat, do you mean?

ZOO. No: why should he cut his throat? He simply dies. He wants to. He is out of countenance, as we call it.

THE ELDERLY GENTLEMAN. Well!!! But suppose he is depraved enough not to want to die, and to settle the difficulty by killing all the rest of you?

ZOO. Oh, he is one of the thoroughly degenerate shortlivers whom we occasionally produce. He emigrates.

THE ELDERLY GENTLEMAN. And what becomes of him then?

ZOO. You shortlived people always think very highly of him. You accept him as what you call a great man.

THE ELDERLY GENTLEMAN. You astonish me; and yet I must admit that what you tell me accounts for a great deal of the little I know of the private life of our great men. We must be very convenient to you as a dumping place for your failures.

ZOO. I admit that.

THE ELDERLY GENTLEMAN. Good. Then if you carry out your plan of colonization, and leave no shortlived countries in the world, what will you do with your undesirables?

ZOO. Kill them. Our tertiaries are not at all squeamish about killing.

THE ELDERLY GENTLEMAN. Gracious Powers!

ZOO. [*glancing up at the sun*] Come. It is just sixteen o'clock; and you have to join your party at half-past in the temple in Galway.

THE ELDERLY GENTLEMAN. [*rising*] Galway! Shall I at last be able to boast of having seen that magnificent city?

ZOO. You will be disappointed: we have no cities. There is a temple of the oracle: that is all.

THE ELDERLY GENTLEMAN. Alas! and I came here to fulfil two long-cherished dreams. One was to see Galway. It has been said, 'See Galway and die.' The other was to contemplate the ruins of London.

ZOO. Ruins! We do not tolerate ruins. Was London a place of any importance?

THE ELDERLY GENTLEMAN. [*amazed*] What! London! It was the mightiest city of antiquity. [*Rhetorically*] Situated just where the Dover Road crosses the Thames, it—

ZOO. [*curtly interrupting*] There is nothing there now. Why should anybody pitch on such a spot to live? The nearest houses are at a place called Strand-on-the-Green: it is very old. Come. We shall go across the water. [*She goes down the steps*].

THE ELDERLY GENTLEMAN. Sic transit gloria mundi!

ZOO. [*from below*] What did you say?

THE ELDERLY GENTLEMAN. [*despairingly*] Nothing. You would not understand. [*He goes down the steps*].

1921

9 RUDY MAREK
Karel Čapek

When the Czech scientist Rudy Marek invents an atomic reactor (the so-called Perfect Karburator), the unintended byproduct of its atom-splitting is the "Absolute." The divine essence that permeates matter, that is to say, is turned loose upon an unsuspecting world; Marek himself develops superhuman physical and mental abilities. The Karburator will cause social, cultural, and economic chaos, resulting in a "Greatest War" of all against all. Prior to this catastrophe, in the first chapters of *The Absolute at Large*, excerpted here, the all-too-human Marek is tempted to make a greedy industrialist the unworthy recipient of his invention's godlike powers.

* * *

The Advertisement

On New Year's Day, 1943, G. H. Bondy, head of the great Metallo-Electric Company, was sitting as usual reading his paper. He skipped the news from the theatre of war rather disrespectfully, avoided the Cabinet crisis, then crowded on sail (for the *People's Journal*, which had grown long ago to five times its ancient size, now afforded enough canvas for an ocean voyage) for the Finance and Commerce section. Here he cruised about for quite a while, then furled his sails, and abandoned himself to his thoughts.

"The Coal Crisis!" he said to himself. "Mines getting worked out; the Ostrava basin suspending work for years.

Heavens above, it's a sheer disaster! We'll have to import Upper Silesian coal. Just work out what that will add to the cost of our manufacturers, and then talk about competition. We're in a pretty fix. And if Germany raises her tariff, we may as well shut up shop. And the Industrial Banks going down, too! What a wretched state of affairs! What a hopeless, stupid, stifling state of affairs! Oh, damn the crisis!"

Here G. H. Bondy, Chairman of the Board of Directors, came to a pause. Something was fidgeting him and would not let him rest. He traced it back to the last page of his discarded newspaper. It was the syllable TION, only part of a word, for the fold of the paper came just in front of the T. It was this very incompleteness which had so curiously impressed itself upon him.

"Well, hang it, it's probably IRON PRODUCTION," Bondy pondered vaguely, "or PREVENTION, or, maybe, RESTITUTION. . . . And the Azote shares have gone down, too. The stagnation's simply shocking. The position's so bad that it's ridiculous. . . . But that's nonsense: who would advertise the RESTITUTION of anything? More likely RESIGNATION. It's sure to be RESIGNATION."

With a touch of annoyance, G. H. Bondy spread out the newspaper to dispose of this irritating word. It had now vanished amid the chequering of the small advertisements. He hunted for it from one column to another, but it had concealed itself with provoking ingenuity. Mr. Bondy then worked from the bottom up, and finally started again from the right-hand side of the page. The contumacious "tion" was not to be found.

Mr. Bondy did not give in. He refolded the paper along its former creases, and behold, the detestable TION leaped forth on the very edge. Keeping his finger firmly on the spot, he swiftly spread the paper out once more, and found——

Mr. Bondy swore under his breath. It was nothing but a very modest, very commonplace small advertisement:

> **INVENTION.**
> Highly remunerative, suitable for any factory, for immediate sale, personal reasons.
> Apply R. Marek, Engineer, Břevnov, 1651.

"So that's all it was!" thought G. H. Bondy. "Some sort of patent braces; just a cheap swindle or some crazy fellow's pet plaything. And here I've wasted five minutes on it! I'm getting scatterbrained myself. What a wretched state of affairs! And not a hint of improvement anywhere!"

He settled himself in a rocking-chair to savour in more comfort the full bitterness of this wretched state of affairs. True, the M.E.C. had ten factories and 34,000 employees. The M.E.C. was the leading producer of iron. The M.E.C. had no competitor as regards boilers. The M.E.C. grates were world-famous. But after thirty years' hard work, gracious Heavens, surely one would have got bigger results elsewhere. . . .

G. H. Bondy sat up with a jerk. "R. Marek, Engineer; R. Marek, Engineer. Half a minute: mightn't that be that red-haired Marek—let's see, what was his name? Rudolph, Rudy Marek, my old chum Rudy of the Technical School? Sure enough, here it is in the advertisement: 'R. Marek, Engineer.' Rudy, you rascal, is it possible? Well, you've not got on very far in the world, my poor fellow! Selling 'a highly remunerative invention.' Ha! ha! '. . . for personal reasons.' We know all about those 'personal reasons.' No money, isn't that what it is? You want to catch some jay of a manufacturer on a nicely limited 'patent,' do you? Oh, well, you always had rather a notion of turning the world upside down. Ah, my lad, where are all our fine notions now! And those extravagant, romantic days when we were young!"

Bondy lay back in his chair once more.

"It's quite likely it really is Marek," he reflected. "Still, Marek had a head for science. He was a bit of a talker, but there was a touch of genius about the lad. He had ideas. In other respects he was a fearfully unpractical fellow. An absolute fool, in fact. It's very surprising that he isn't a Professor," mused Mr. Bondy. "I haven't set eyes on him for twenty years. God knows what he has been up to; perhaps he's come right down in the world. Yes, he must be down and out, living away over in Břevnov, poor chap . . . and getting a living out of inventions! What an awful finish!"

He tried to imagine the straits of the fallen inventor. He managed to picture a horribly shaggy and dishevelled head, surrounded by dismal paper walls like those in a film. There is no furniture, only a mattress in the corner, and a pitiful model made of spools, nails, and matchends on the table. A murky window looks out on a little yard. Upon this scene of unspeakable indigence enters a visitor in rich furs. "I have come to have a look at your invention." The half-blind inventor fails to recognize his old schoolfellow. He humbly bows his tousled head, looks about for a seat to offer to his guest, and then, oh Heaven! with his poor, stiff, shaking fingers he tries to get his sorry invention going—it's some crazy perpetual motion device—and mumbles confusedly that it should work, and certainly *would* work, if only he had . . . if only he could buy. . . . The fur-coated visitor looks all around the garret, and suddenly he takes a leather wallet from his pocket and lays on the table one, two (Mr. Bondy takes fright and cries "That's enough!") three thousand-crown notes. ("One would have been quite enough . . . to go on with, I mean," protests something in Mr. Bondy's brain.)

"There is . . . something to carry on the work with, Mr. Marek. No, no, you're not in any way indebted to me. Who am I? That doesn't matter. Just take it that I am a friend."

Bondy found this scene very pleasant and touching.

"I'll send my secretary to Marek," he resolved; "tomorrow without fail. And what shall I do today? It's a holiday; I'm not going to the works. My time's my own . . . a wretched state things are in! Nothing to do all day long! Suppose I went round to-day myself."

G. H. Bondy hesitated. It would be a bit of an adventure to go and see for oneself how that queer fellow was struggling along in Břevnov.

"After all, we were such chums! And old times have their claim on one. Yes, I'll go!" decided Mr. Bondy. And he went.

He had rather a boring time while his car was gliding all over Břevnov in search of a mean hovel bearing the number 1651. They had to inquire at the police-station.

"Marek, Marek," said the inspector, searching his memory. "That must be Marek the engineer, of Marek and Co., the electric lamp factory, 1651, Mixa Street."

The electric lamp factory! Bondy felt disappointed, even annoyed. Rudy Marek wasn't living up in a garret, then! He was a manufacturer and wanted to sell some invention or other "for personal reasons." If that didn't smell of bankruptcy, his name wasn't Bondy.

"Do you happen to know how Mr. Marek is doing?" he asked the police inspector, with a casual air, as he took his seat in the car.

"Oh, splendidly!" the inspector answered. "He's got a very fine business." Local pride made him add, "The firm's very well known"; and he amplified this with: "A very wealthy man, and a learned one, too. He does nothing but make experiments."

"Mixa Street!" cried Bondy to his chauffeur.

"Third on the right!" the inspector called after the car.

Bondy was soon ringing at the residential part of quite a pretty little factory.

"It's all very nice and clean here," he remarked to himself. "Flower-beds in the yard, creeper on the walls. Humph! There always was a touch of the philanthropist and reformer about that confounded Marek." And at that moment Marek himself came out on the steps to meet him; Rudy Marek, awfully thin and serious-looking, up in the clouds, so to speak. It gave Bondy a queer pang to find him neither so young as he used to be nor so unkempt as that inventor; so utterly different from what Bondy had imagined that he was scarcely recognizable. But before he could fully realize his disillusionment, Marek stretched out his hand and said quietly, "Well, so you've come at last, Bondy! I've been expecting you!"

The Karburator

"I've been expecting you!" Marek repeated, when he had seated his guest in a comfortable leather chair. Nothing on earth would have induced Bondy to own up to his vision of the fallen inventor. "Just fancy!" he said, with a rather forced gaiety. "What a coincidence! It struck me only this very morning that we hadn't seen one another for twenty years. Twenty years, Rudy, think of it!"

"Hm," said Marek. "And so you want to buy my invention."

"Buy it?" said G. H. Bondy hesitatingly. "I really don't know . . . I haven't even given it a thought. I wanted to see you and——"

"Oh, come, you needn't pretend," Marek interrupted him. "I knew that you were coming. You'd be sure to, for a thing like this. This kind of invention is just in your line. There's a lot to be done with it." He made an eloquent motion with his hand, coughed, and began again more deliberately. "The invention I am going to show you means a bigger revolution in technical methods than Watt's invention of the steam-engine. To give you its nature briefly, it provides, putting it theoretically, for the *complete utilization of atomic energy*."

Bondy concealed a yawn. "But tell me, what have you been doing all these twenty years?"

Marek glanced at him with some surprise.

"Modern science teaches that all matter—that is to say, its atoms—is composed of a vast number of units of energy. An atom is in reality a collection of electrons, *i.e.* of the tiniest particles of electricity."

"That's tremendously interesting," Bondy broke in. "I was always weak in physics, you know. But you're not looking well, Marek. By the way, how did you happen to come by this plaything . . . this, er . . . factory?"

"I? Oh, quite by accident. I invented a new kind of filament for electric bulbs. . . . But that's nothing; I only came upon it incidentally. You see, for twenty years I've been working on the combustion of matter. Tell me yourself, Bondy, what is the greatest problem of modern industry?"

"Doing business," said Bondy. "And are you married yet?"

"I'm a widower," answered Marek, leaping up excitedly. "No, business has nothing to do with it, I tell you. It's combustion. The complete utilization of the heat-energy contained in matter! Just consider that we use hardly one hundred-thousandth of the heat that there is in coal, and that could be extracted from it! Do you realize that!"

"Yes, coal is terribly dear!" said Mr. Bondy sapiently.

Marek sat down and cried disgustedly, "Look here, if you haven't come here about my Karburator, Bondy, you can go."

"Go ahead, then," Bondy returned, anxious to conciliate him.

Marek rested his head in his hands, and after a struggle came out with, "For twenty years I've been working on it, and now—now, I'll sell it to the first man who comes along! My magnificent dream! The greatest invention of all the ages! Seriously, Bondy, I tell you, it's something really amazing."

"No doubt, in the present wretched state of affairs," assented Bondy.

"No, without any qualification at all, amazing. Do you realize that it means the utilization of atomic energy without any residue whatever?"

"Aha," said Bondy. "So we're going to do our heating with atoms. Well, why not? . . . You've got a nice place here, Rudy. Small and pleasant. How many hands do you employ?"

Marek took no notice. "You know," he said thoughtfully, "it's all the same thing, whatever you call it—the utilization of atomic energy, or the complete combustion of matter, or the disintegration of matter. You can call it what you please."

"I'm in favour of 'combustion'!" said Mr. Bondy. "It sounds more familiar."

"But 'disintegration' is more exact—to break up the atoms into electrons, and harness the electrons and make them work. Do you understand that?"

"Perfectly," Bondy assured him. "The point is to harness them!"

"Well, imagine, say, that there are two horses at the ends of a rope, pulling with all their might in opposite directions. Do you know what you have then?"

"Some kind of sport, I suppose," suggested Mr. Bondy.

"No, a state of repose. The horses pull, but they stay where they are. And if you were to cut the rope——"

"—The horses would fall over," cried G. H. Bondy, with a flash of inspiration.

"No, but they would start running; they would become energy released. Now, pay attention. Matter is a team in that very position. Cut the bonds that hold its electrons together, and they will . . ."

"Run loose!"

"Yes, but we can catch and harness them, don't you see? Or put it to yourself this way: we burn a piece of coal, say, to produce heat. We do get a little heat from it, but we also get ashes, coal-gas, and soot. So we don't lose the matter altogether, do we?"

"No.—Won't you have a cigar?"

"No, I won't.—But the matter which is left still contains a vast quantity of unused atomic energy. If we used up the whole of the atomic energy, we should use up the whole of the atoms. In short, *the matter would vanish altogether*."

"Aha! Now I understand."

"It's just as though we were to grind corn badly—as if we ground up the thin outer husk and threw the rest away, just as we throw away ashes. When the grinding is perfect, there's nothing or next to nothing left of the grain, is there? In the same way, when there is perfect combustion, there's nothing or next to nothing left of the matter we burn. It's ground up completely. It is used up. It returns to its original nothingness. You know, it takes a tremendous amount of energy to make matter exist at all. Take away its existence, compel it not to be, and you thereby release an enormous supply of power. That's how it is, Bondy."

"Aha. That's not bad."

"Pflüger, for instance, calculates that one kilogramme of coal contains twenty-three billions of calories. I think that Pflüger exaggerates."

"Decidedly."

"I have arrived at seven billions myself, theoretically. But even that signifies that one kilogramme of coal, if it underwent complete combustion, would run a good-sized factory for several hundred hours!"

"The devil it does!" cried Mr. Bondy, springing from his chair.

"I can't give you the exact number of hours. I've been burning half a kilogramme of coal for six weeks at a pressure of thirty kilogrammetres and, man alive," said the engineer in a whisper, turning pale, "it's still going on . . . and on . . . and on."

Bondy was embarrassed; he stroked his smooth round chin. "Listen, Marek," he began, hesitatingly. "You're surely . . . er . . . a bit . . . er . . . overworked."

Marek's hand thrust the suggestion aside. "Not a bit of it. If you'd only get up physics a bit, I could give you an explanation of my Karburator* in which the combustion

---

*This name which Marek gave to his atomic boiler is, of course, quite incorrect, and is one of the melancholy results of the ignorance of Latin among technicians. A more exact term would have been Komburator, Atomic Kettle, Karbowatt, Disintegrator, Motor M, Bondymover, Hylergon, Molecular Disintegration Dynamo, E. W., and other designations which were later proposed. It was, of course, the bad one that was generally adopted.

takes place. It involves a whole chapter of advanced physics, you know. But you'll see it downstairs in the cellar. I shovelled half a kilogramme of coal into the machine, then I shut it up and had it officially sealed in the presence of witnesses, so that no one could put any more coal in. Go and have a look at it for yourself—go on—go now! You won't understand it, anyway, but—go down to the cellar! Go on down, man, I tell you!"

"Won't you come with me?" asked Bondy in astonishment.

"No, you go alone. And . . . I say, Bondy . . . don't stay down there long."

"Why not?" asked Bondy, growing a trifle suspicious.

"Oh, nothing much. Only I've a notion that perhaps it's not quite healthy down there. Turn on the light, the switch is just by the door. That noise down in the cellar doesn't come from my machine. It works noiselessly, steadily, and without any smell. . . . The roaring is only a . . . a ventilator. Well, now, you go on. I'll wait here. Then you can tell me . . ."

*

Bondy went down the cellar steps, quite glad to be away from that madman for a while (quite mad, no doubt whatever about it) and rather worried as to the quickest means of getting out of the place altogether. Why, just look, the cellar had a huge thick reinforced door just like an armour-plated safe in a bank. And now let's have a light. The switch was just by the door. And there in the middle of the arched concrete cellar, clean as a monastery cell, lay a gigantic copper cylinder resting on cement supports. It was closed on all sides except at the top, where there was a grating bedecked with seals. Inside the machine all was darkness and silence. With a smooth and regular motion the cylinder thrust forth a piston which slowly rotated a heavy fly-wheel. That was all. Only the ventilator in the cellar window kept up a ceaseless rattle.

Perhaps it was the draught from the ventilator or something—but Mr. Bondy felt a peculiar breeze upon his brow, and an eerie sensation as though his hair were standing on end; and then it seemed as if he were being borne through boundless space; and then as though he were floating in the air without any sensation of his own weight. G. H. Bondy fell on his knees, lost in a bewildering, shining ecstasy. He felt as if he must shout and sing, he seemed to hear about him the rustle of unceasing and innumerable wings. And suddenly someone seized him violently by the hand and dragged him from the cellar. It was Marek, wearing over his head a mask or a helmet like a diver's, and he hauled Bondy up the stairs.

Up in the room he pulled off his metal head-covering and wiped away the sweat that soaked his brow.

"Only just in time," he gasped, showing tremendous agitation.

Pantheism

G.H. Bondy felt rather as though he were dreaming. Marek settled him in an easy chair with quite maternal solicitude, and made haste to bring some brandy.

"Here, drink this up quickly," he jerked out hoarsely, offering him the glass with a trembling hand. "You came over queer down there too, didn't you?"

"On the contrary," Bondy answered unsteadily. "It was . . . it was beautiful, old chap! I felt as if I were flying, or something like that."

"Yes, yes," said Marek quickly. "That's exactly what I mean. As though you were flying along, or rather soaring upward, wasn't that it?"

"It was a feeling of perfect bliss," said Mr. Bondy. "I think it's what you'd call being transported. As if there was something down there . . . something . . ."

"Something—holy?" asked Marek hesitatingly.

"Perhaps. Yes, man alive, you're right. I never go to church, Rudy, never in my life, but down in that cellar I felt as if I were in church. Tell me, man, what did I do down there?"

"You went on your knees," Marek muttered with a bitter smile, and began striding up and down the room.

Bondy stroked his bald head in bewilderment.

"That's extraordinary. But come, on my knees? Well, then, tell me what . . . what is there in the cellar that acts on one so queerly?"

"The Karburator," growled Marek, gnawing his lips. His cheeks seemed even more sunken than before, and were as pale as death.

"But, confound it, man," cried Bondy in amazement, "how can it be?"

The engineer only shrugged his shoulders, and with bent head went on pacing up and down the room.

G. H. Bondy's eyes followed him with childish astonishment. "The man's crazy," he said to himself. "All the same, what the devil is it that comes over one in that cellar? That tormenting bliss, that tremendous security, that terror, that overwhelming feeling of devotion, or whatever you like to call it." Mr. Bondy arose and poured himself out another dash of brandy.

"I say, Marek," he said, "I've got it now."

"Got what?" exclaimed Marek, halting.

"That business in the cellar. That queer psychical condition. It's some form of poisoning, isn't it? . . ."

Marek gave an angry laugh. "Oh, yes, of course, poisoning!"

"I thought so at once," declared Bondy, his mind at rest in an instant. "That apparatus of yours produces something, ah . . . er . . . something like ozone, doesn't it? Or more likely poisonous gas. And when anyone inhales it, it . . . er . . . poisons him or excites him somehow, isn't that it? Why, of course, man, it's nothing but poisonous gases; they're probably given off somehow by the combustion of the coal in that . . . that Karburator of yours. Some sort of illuminating gas or paradise gas, or phosgene or something of the sort. That's why you've put in the ventilator, and that's why you wear a gas-mask when you go into the cellar, isn't it? Just some confounded gases."

"If only there were nothing but *gases*!" Marek burst out, shaking his fists threateningly. "Look here, Bondy, that's why I must sell that Karburator! I simply can't stand it—I can't stand it . . . *I can't stand it*," he shouted, well-nigh weeping. "I never dreamed my Karburator would do anything like *this* . . . this . . . terrifying mischief! Just think, it's been going on like *that* from the very beginning! And every one feels it who comes near the thing. You haven't any notion even yet, Bondy. But our porter caught it properly."

"Poor fellow!" said the astonished Bondy, full of sympathy. "And did he die of it?"

"No, but he got *converted*," cried Marek in despair. "Bondy, you're a man I can confide in. My invention, my Karburator, has one terrible defect. Nevertheless, you're going to buy it or else take it from me as a gift. You will, Bondy—even if it spews forth demons. It doesn't matter to you, Bondy, so long as you can get your millions out of it. And you'll get them, man. It's a stupendous thing, I tell you. . . . But I don't want to have anything more to do with it. You haven't such a sensitive conscience as I have, you know, Bondy. It'll bring in millions, thousands of millions; but it will lay a frightful load upon your conscience. Make up your mind!"

"Oh, leave me alone," Mr. Bondy protested. "If it gives off poisonous gases, the authorities will prohibit it, and there's an end of it. You know the wretched state of affairs here. Now in America . . ."

"It isn't poisonous gases," Marek exclaimed. "It's *something a thousand times worse*. Mark what I tell you, Bondy, it's something beyond human reason, but there's not a scrap of deception about it. Well, then, my Karburator actually does burn up matter, causes its utter combustion, so that not even a grain of dust remains. Or rather, it breaks it up, crushes it, splits it up into electrons, consumes it, grinds it—I don't know how to express it—in short, uses it up completely. You have no idea what a colossal amount of energy is contained in the atoms. With half a hundredweight of coal in the Karburator you can sail right round the world in a steamship, you can light the whole city of Prague, you can supply power for the whole of a huge factory, or anything you like. A bit of coal the size of a nut will do the heating and the cooking for a whole family. And ultimately we shan't even require coal; we can do our heating with the first pebble or handful of dirt we pick up in front of the house. Every scrap of matter has in it more energy than an enormous boiler; you've only to extract it. You've only to know how to secure total combustion! Well, Bondy, I can do it; my Karburator can do it. You'll admit, Bondy, that it has been worthwhile toiling over it for twenty years."

"Look here, Rudy," Bondy began slowly, "it's all very extraordinary—but I believe you, so to speak. On my soul, I do believe you. You know, when I stood in front of that Karburator of yours, I felt that I was in the presence of something overpoweringly great, something a man could not withstand. I can't help it: I believe you. Down there in the cellar you have something uncanny, something that will overturn the whole world."

"Alas, Bondy," Marek whispered anxiously, "that's just where the trouble is. Listen, and I'll tell you the whole thing. Have you ever read Spinoza?"

"No."

"No more had I. But now, you see, I am beginning to read that sort of thing. I don't understand it—it's terribly difficult stuff for us technical people—but there's something in it. Do you by any chance believe in God?"

"I? Well, now . . ." G. H. Bondy deliberated. "Upon my word, I couldn't say. Perhaps there is a God, but He's on some other planet. Not on ours. Oh, well, that sort of thing doesn't fit in with our times at all. Tell me, what makes you drag that into it?"

"I don't believe in anything," said Marek in a hard voice. "I don't want to believe. I have always been an atheist. I believed in matter and in progress and in nothing else. I'm a scientific man, Bondy; and science cannot admit the existence of God."

"From the business point of view," Mr. Bondy remarked, "it's a matter of indifference. If He wants to exist, in Heaven's name, let Him. We aren't mutually exclusive."

"But from the scientific point of view, Bondy," cried the engineer sternly, "it is absolutely intolerable. It's a case of Him or science. I don't assert that God does not exist; I only assert that He *ought* not to exist, or at least ought not to let Himself be seen. And I believe that science is crowding Him out step by step, or at any rate is preventing Him from letting Himself be seen; and I believe that that is the greatest mission of science."

"Possibly," said Bondy calmly. "But go on."

"And now just imagine, Bondy, that. . . . But wait, I'll put it to you this way. Do you know what Pantheism is? It's the belief that God, or the Absolute, if you prefer it, is manifest in everything that exists. In men, as in stones, in the grass, the water—everywhere. And do you know what Spinoza teaches? That matter is only the outward manifestation, only one phase of the divine substance, the other phase of which is spirit. And do you know what Fechner teaches?"

"No, I don't," the other admitted.

"Fechner teaches that everything, everything that is, is penetrated with the divine, that God fills with His being the whole of the matter in the world. And do you know Leibniz? Leibniz teaches that physical matter is composed of psychical atoms, monads, whose nature is divine. What do you say to that?"

"I don't know," said G. H. Bondy. "I don't understand it."

"Nor do I. It's fearfully abstruse. But let us assume, for the sake of argument, that God is contained in all forms of physical matter, that He is, as it were, imprisoned in it. And when you smash this matter up completely, He flies out of it as though from a box. He is suddenly set free. He is released from matter as illuminating gas is from coal. You have only to burn one single atom up completely, and immediately the whole cellar is filled with the Absolute. It's simply appalling how quickly it spreads."

"Hold on," Mr. Bondy interrupted. "Say that all over again, but say it slowly."

"Look at it like this then," said Marek. "We're assuming that all matter contains the Absolute in some state of confinement. We can call it a latent imprisoned force, or simply say that as God is omnipresent He is therefore present in all matter and in every particle of matter. And now suppose you utterly destroy a piece of matter, apparently leaving not the slightest residue. Then, since all matter is really Matter plus Absolute, what you have destroyed is only the matter, and you're left with an indestructible residue—free and active Absolute. You're left with the chemically unanalysable, immaterial residue, which shows no spectrum lines, neither atomic weight nor chemical affinity, no obedience to Boyle's law, none, none whatever, of the properties of matter. What is left behind is pure God. A chemical nullity which acts with monstrous energy. Being immaterial, it is not subject to the laws of matter. Thence, it already follows that its manifestations are contrary to nature and downright miraculous. All this proceeds from the assumption that God is present in all matter. Can you imagine, for the sake of argument, that He is really so present?"

"I certainly can," said Bondy. "What then?"

"Good," said Marek, rising to his feet. "Then *it's the solemn truth*."

God in the Cellar

G.H. Bondy sucked meditatively at his cigar. "And how did you find it out, old chap?" he asked at last.

"By the effect on myself," said the engineer, resuming his march up and down the room. "As a result of its complete disintegration of matter, my Perfect Karburator manufactures a by-product: pure and unconfined Absolute, God in a chemically pure form. At one end, so to speak, it emits mechanical power, and at the other, the divine principle. Just as when you split water up into hydrogen and oxygen, only on an immensely larger scale."

"Hm," said Mr. Bondy. "And then—?"

"I've an idea," continued Marek cautiously, "that there are many of the elect who can separate the material substance in themselves from the divine substance. They can release or distill the Absolute, as it were, from their material selves. Christ and the miracle-workers, fakirs, mediums, and prophets have achieved it by means of their psychic power. My Karburator does it by a purely mechanical process. It acts, you might say, as a factory for the Absolute."

"Facts," said G. H. Bondy. "Stick to facts."

"These are facts. I constructed my Perfect Karburator only in theory to begin with. Then I made a little model, which wouldn't go. The fourth model was the first that really worked. It was only about so big, but it ran quite nicely. But even while I was working with it on this small scale, I felt peculiar physical effects—a strange exhilaration—a 'fey' feeling. But I thought it was due to being so pleased about the invention, or to being overworked, perhaps. It was then that I first began to prophesy and perform miracles."

"To do *what*?" Bondy cried.

"To prophesy and perform miracles," Marek repeated gloomily. "I had moments of astounding illumination. I saw, for instance, quite clearly, things that would happen in the future. I predicted even your visit here. And once I tore my nail off on a lathe. I looked at the damaged finger, and all at once a new nail grew on it. Very likely I'd formed the wish, but all the same it's queer and . . . terrible. Another time—just think of it—I rose right up into the air. It's called levitation, you know. I never believed in any rubbish of that kind, so you can imagine the shock it gave me."

"I can quite believe it," said Bondy gravely. "It must be most distressing."

"Extremely distressing. I thought it must be due to nerves, a kind of auto-suggestion or something. In the meanwhile I erected the big Karburator in the cellar and started it off. As I told you, it's been running now for six weeks, day and night. And it was there that I first realized the full significance of the business. In a single day the cellar was chock-full of the Absolute, ready to burst with it; and it began to spread all over the house. The pure Absolute penetrates all matter, you know, but it takes a little longer with solid substances. In the air it spread as swiftly as light. When I went in, I tell you, man, it took me like a stroke. I shrieked out aloud. I don't know where I got the strength to run away. When I got upstairs, I thought over the whole business. My first notion was that it must be some new intoxicating, stimulating gas, developed by the process of complete combustion. That's why I had that ventilator fixed up, from the outside. Two of the fitters on the job 'saw the light' and had visions; the third was a drinker and so perhaps to some extent immune. As long as I thought it was only a gas, I made a series of experiments with it, and it's interesting to find that any light burns much more brightly in the Absolute. If it would let itself be confined in glass bulbs, I'd fill lamps with it; but it escapes from any vessel, however thick you make it. Then I decided it must be some sort of Ultra-X-ray, but there's no trace of any form of electricity, and it makes no impression on photo-sensitive plates. On the third day, the porter and his wife, who live just over the cellar, had to be taken off to the sanatorium."

"What for?" asked Bondy.

"He got religion. He was inspired. He gave religious addresses and performed miracles. His wife uttered prophecies. My porter had been a thoroughly hard-headed chap, a monist and a freethinker, and an unusually steady fellow. Well, just fancy, from no visible cause whatever, he started healing people by laying on of hands. Of course, Bondy, he was reported at once. The district health officer, who is a friend of mine, was tremendously upset about it; so, to avoid any scandal, I had the porter sent to a sanatorium. They say he's better now; quite cured. He has lost the power to perform miracles. I'm going to send him on the land to recuperate. . . . Then I began to work miracles myself and see into the future. Among other things, I had visions of gigantic, swampy primeval forests, overgrown with mosses and inhabited by weird monsters—probably because the Karburator was burning Upper Silesian coal, which is of the oldest formation. Possibly the God of the Carboniferous Age is in it."

Mr. Bondy shuddered. "Marek, this is frightful!"

"It is indeed," said Marek sorrowfully. "Gradually I began to see that it wasn't gas, but the Absolute. The symptoms were terrible. I could read people's thoughts, light emanated from me, I had a desperate struggle not to become absorbed in prayer and preach belief in God. I tried to clog the Karburator up with sand, but I was seized with a bout of levitation. That machine won't let anything stop it. I don't sleep at home nowadays. Even in the factory there have been several serious cases of illumination among the workmen. I don't know where to turn, Bondy. Yes, I've tried every possible isolating material that might prevent the Absolute from getting out of the cellar. Ashes, sand, metal walls, nothing can keep it back. I've even tried covering the cellar with the work of Professor Krejčí, Spencer, Haeckel, and all the Positivists you can think of: would you believe it, the Absolute goes calmly through even that stuff! Even papers, prayer-books, Lives of the Saints, Patriotic Song-books, university lectures, bestsellers, political treatises, and Parliamentary Reports, present no obstacle to it. I'm simply desperate. You can't shut it up, you can't soak it up. It's mischief let loose."

"Oh, but why?" said Mr. Bondy. "Does it really mean such mischief? Even if all this were true . . . is it such a disaster?"

"Bondy, my Karburator is a terrific thing. It will overturn the whole world, mechanically and socially. It will cheapen production to an unbelievable extent. It will do away with poverty and hunger. It will some day save our planet from freezing up. But, on the other hand, it hurls God as a by-product into the world. I implore you, Bondy, don't underrate what it means. We aren't used to reckoning with God as a *reality*. We don't know what His presence may bring about—say, socially, morally, and so on. Why, man, this thing affects the whole of human civilization!"

"Wait a minute!" said Bondy thoughtfully. "Perhaps there's some charm or other that would exorcise it. Have you called in the clergy?"

"What kind of clergy?"

"Any kind. The denomination probably makes no difference in this case, you know. Perhaps they could do something to stop it."

"Oh, that's all superstition!" burst out Marek. "Leave me alone with your parsons! Catch me giving them a chance to make a miraculous shrine out of my cellar! Me, with my views!"

"Very well," declared Mr. Bondy. "Then I'll call them in myself. You never can tell. . . . Come, it can't do any harm, anyway. After all, I haven't anything against God. Only He oughtn't to interfere with business. Have you tried negotiating with Him in a friendly spirit?"

"No," admitted the engineer.

"That was a mistake," said Bondy dryly. "Perhaps you could come to some agreement with Him. A proper formal contract, in something like this style: 'We guarantee to produce You discreetly and continuously to an extent to be fixed by mutual agreement; in return for which You pledge yourself to refrain from any divine manifestations within such and such a radius from the place of origin.' What do you think—would He consider these terms?"

"I don't know," answered Marek uneasily. "He seems to have a decided inclination in favour of becoming independent of matter once more. Still, perhaps . . . in His own interests . . . He might be willing to listen. But don't ask me to do it."

"Very well, then!" Bondy agreed. "I'll send my own solicitor. A very tactful and capable fellow. And then again . . . er . . . one might perhaps offer Him some church or other. After all, a factory cellar and its surroundings are rather . . . well . . . undignified quarters for Him. We ought to ascertain His tastes. Have you tried yet?"

"No; it would suit me best to flood the cellar with water."

"Gently, Marek, gently. I'm probably going to buy this invention. You understand, of course, that . . . I'll send my experts over first . . . we'll have to look into the business a little further. Perhaps it's only poisonous fumes, after all. And if it actually turns out to be God Himself, that's all right. So long as the Karburator really works."

Marek got up. "And you wouldn't be afraid to install the Karburator in the M.E.C. works?"

"I'm not afraid," said Bondy, rising, "to manufacture Karburators wholesale. Karburators for trains and ships. Karburators for central heating, for houses, offices, factories, and schools. In ten years' time all the heating in the world will be done by Karburators. I'll give you three per cent. of the gross profits. The first year it will only be a few millions, perhaps. Meanwhile you can move out, so that I can send my men along. I'll bring the Suffragan Bishop up to-morrow morning. See that you keep out of his way, Rudy. I don't like seeing you about here in any case. You are rather abrupt, and I don't want to offend the Absolute to start with."

"Bondy," Marek whispered, horror-stricken. "I warn you for the last time. It means letting God loose upon this world!"

"Then," said G. H. Bondy, with dignity, "He will be personally indebted to me to that extent. And I hope that He won't show me any ill-feeling."

1922

10 ZUANTHROL

Edgar Rice Burroughs

When Tarzan of the Apes crash-lands an airplane in West Africa's Great Thorn Forest, he encounters the Minunians—a lost race of white-skinned people, four times smaller than himself, divided into warring states. Komodoflorensal, a Trohanadalmakusian, teaches Tarzan the Minuni language . . . shortly before they are captured by the Veltopismakusians. Using vibratory technology, Zoanthrohago, a *walmak*—a wizard, or "scientist who works miracles"—reduces Tarzan to Minunian size! Sardonically dubbed Zuanthrol ("giant"), Tarzan will discover that he still possesses his full-sized strength . . . making him a superhuman of sorts. In the scene excerpted here, the *walmak* explains his science to King Elkomoelhago.

* * *

Zoanthrohago bowed. "And now," he said, "to the discussion of our experiments, which we hope will reveal a method for increasing the stature of our warriors when they go forth to battle with our enemies, and of reducing them to normal size once more when they return."

"I hate the mention of battles," cried the king, with a shudder.

"But we must be prepared to win them when they are forced upon us," suggested Zoanthrohago.

"I suppose so," assented the king; "but once we perfect this method of ours we shall need but a few warriors and the rest may be turned to peaceful and useful occupations. However, go on with the discussion."

Zoanthrohago concealed a smile, and rising, walked around the end of the table and stopped beside the ape-man. "Here," he said, placing a finger at the base of Tarzan's skull, "there lies, as you know, a small, oval, reddish gray body containing a liquid which influences the growth of tissues and organs. It long ago occurred to me that interference with the normal functioning of this gland would alter the growth of the subject to which it belonged. I experimented with small rodents and achieved remarkable results; but the thing I wished to accomplish, the increase of man's stature I have been unable to achieve. I have tried many methods and some day I shall discover the right one. I think I am on the right track, and that it is merely now a matter of experimentation. You know that stroking your face lightly with a smooth bit of stone produces a pleasurable sensation. Apply the same stone to the same face in the same manner, but with greatly increased force and you produce a diametrically opposite sensation. Rub the stone slowly across the face and back again many times, and then repeat the same motion rapidly for the same number of times and you will discover that the results are quite different. I am that close to a solution; I have the correct method but not quite, as yet, the correct application. I can reduce creatures in size, but I cannot enlarge them; and although I can reduce them with great ease, I cannot determine the period or endurance of their reduction. In some cases, subjects have not regained their normal size under thirty-nine moons, and in others, they have done so in as short a period as three moons. There have been cases where normal stature was regained gradually during a period of seven suns, and others where the subject passed suddenly from a reduced size to normal size in less than a hundred heart-beats; this latter phenomenon being always accompanied by fainting and unconsciousness when it occurred during waking hours."

"Of course," commented Elkomoelhago. "Now, let us see. I believe the thing is simpler than you imagine. You say that to reduce the size of this subject you struck him with a rock upon the base of the skull. Therefore, to enlarge his size, the most natural and scientific thing to do would be to strike him a similar blow upon the forehead. Fetch the rock and we will prove the correctness of my theory."

For a moment Zoanthrohago was at a loss as to how best to circumvent the stupid intention of the king without humiliating his pride and arousing his resentment; but the courtiers of Elkomoelhago were accustomed to think quickly in similar emergencies and Zoanthrohago speedily found an avenue of escape from his dilemma.

"Your sagacity is the pride of your people, Thagosoto," he said, "and your brilliant hyperbole the despair of your courtiers. In a clever figure of speech you suggest the way to achievement. By reversing the manner in which we reduced the stature of Zuanthrol we should be able to increase it; but, alas, I have tried this and failed. But wait, let us repeat the experiment precisely as it was originally carried out and then, by reversing it, we shall, perhaps, be enabled to determine why I have failed in the past."

He stepped quickly across the room to one of a series of large cupboards that lined the wall and opening the door of it revealed a cage in which were a number of rodents. Selecting one of these he returned to the table, where, with wooden pegs and bits of cord he fastened the rodent securely to a smooth board, its legs spread out and its body flattened, the underside of the lower jaw resting firmly upon a small metal plate set flush with the surface of the board. He then brought forth a small wooden box and a large metal disc, the latter mounted vertically between supports that permitted it to be revolved rapidly by means of a hand crank. Mounted rigidly upon the same axis as the revolving disc was another which remained stationary. The latter disc appeared to have been constructed of seven segments, each of a different material from all the others, and from each of these segments a pad, or brush, protruded sufficiently to press lightly against the revolving disc.

To the reverse side of each of the seven segments of the stationary disc a wire was attached, and these wires Zoanthrohago now connected to seven posts projecting from the upper surface of the wooden box. A single wire attached to a post upon the side of the box had at its other extremity a small, curved metal plate attached to the inside of a leather collar. This collar Zoanthrohago adjusted about the neck of the rodent so that the metal plate came in contact with its skin at the base of the skull and as close to the hypophysis gland as possible.

He then turned his attention once more to the wooden box, upon the top of which, in addition to the seven binding posts, was a circular instrument consisting of a dial about the periphery of which were a series of hieroglyphics. From the center of this dial projected seven tubular, concentric shafts, each of which supported a needle, which was shaped or painted in some distinguishing manner, while beneath the dial seven small metal discs were set in the cover of the box so that they lay in the arc of a circle from the center of which a revolving metal shaft was so arranged that its free end might be moved to any one of the seven metal discs at the will of the operator.

The connections having all been made, Zoanthrohago moved the free end of the shaft from one of the metal discs to another, keeping his eyes at all times intently upon the dial, the seven needles of which moved variously as he shifted the shaft from point to point.

Elkomoelhago was an intent, if somewhat bewildered, observer, and the slave, Zuanthrol, unobserved, had moved nearer the table that he might better watch this experiment which might mean so much to him.

Zoanthrohago continued to manipulate the revolving shaft and the needles moved hither and thither from one series of hieroglyphics to another, until at last the *walmak* appeared satisfied.

"It is not always easy," he said, "to attune the instrument to the frequency of the organ upon which we are working. From all matter and even from such incorporeal a thing as thought there emanate identical particles, so infinitesimal as to be scarce noted by the most delicate of my instruments. These particles constitute the basic structure of all things whether animate or inanimate, corporeal or incorporeal. The frequency, quantity and rhythm of the emanations determine the nature of the substance. Having located upon this dial the coefficient of the gland under discussion it now becomes necessary, in order to so interfere with its proper functioning that the growth of the creature involved will be not only stopped but actually reversed, that we decrease the frequency, increase the quantity and compound the rhythm of these emanations. This I shall now proceed to do," and he forthwith manipulated several small buttons upon one side of the box, and grasping the crankhandle of the free disc revolved it rapidly.

The result was instantaneous and startling. Before their eyes Elkomoelhago, the king, and Zuanthrol, the slave, saw the rodent shrink rapidly in size, while retaining its proportions unchanged. Tarzan, who had followed every move and every word of the *walmak*, leaned far over that he might impress indelibly upon his memory the position of the seven needles. Elkomoelhago glanced up and discovered his interest.

"We do not need this fellow now," he said, addressing Zoanthrohago. "Have him sent away."

"Yes, Thagosoto," replied Zoanthrohago, summoning a warrior whom he directed to remove Tarzan and Komodoflorensal to a chamber where they could be secured until their presence was again required.

*

Through several chambers and corridors they were conducted toward the center of the dome on the same level as the chamber in which they had left the king and the *walmak* until finally they were thrust into a small chamber and a heavy door slammed and barred behind them.

There was no candle in the chamber. A faint light, however, relieved the darkness so that the interior of the room was discernible. The chamber contained two benches and a table—that was all. The light which faintly illuminated it entered through a narrow embrasure which was heavily barred, but it was evidently daylight.

"We are alone," whispered Komodoflorensal, "and at last we can converse; but we must be cautious," he added. "'Trust not too far the loyalty of even the stones of your chamber!'" he quoted.

"Where are we?" asked Tarzan. "You are more familiar with Minunian dwellings than I."

"We are upon the highest level of the Royal Dome of Elkomoelhago," replied the prince. "With no such informality does a king visit the other domes of his city. You may rest assured that this is Elkomoelhago's. We are in one of the innermost chambers, next the central shaft that pierces the dome from its lowest level to its roof. For this reason we do not need a candle to support life—we will obtain sufficient air through this embrasure. And now, tell me what happened within the room with Elkomoelhago and Zoanthrohago."

"I discovered how they reduced my stature," replied Tarzan, "and, furthermore, that at almost any time I may regain my full size—an occurrence that may eventuate from three to thirty-nine moons after the date of my reduction. Even Zoanthrohago cannot determine when this thing will happen."

"Let us hope that it does not occur while you are in this small chamber," exclaimed Komodoflorensal.

"I would have a devil of a time getting out," agreed Tarzan.

"You would never get out," his friend assured him. "While you might, before your reduction, have crawled through some of the larger corridors upon the first level, or even upon many of the lower levels, you could not squeeze into the smaller corridors of the upper levels, which are reduced in size as the necessity for direct supports for the roof increase as we approach the apex of the dome."

"Then it behooves me to get out of here as quickly as possible," said Tarzan.

Komodoflorensal shook his head. "Hope is a beautiful thing, my friend," he said, "but if you were a Minunian you would know that under such circumstances as we find ourselves it is a waste of mental energy. Look at these bars," and he walked to the window and shook the heavy irons that spanned the embrasure. "Think you that you could negotiate these?"

"I haven't examined them," replied the ape-man, "but I shall never give up hope of escaping; that your people do is doubtless the principal reason that they remain forever in bondage. You are too much a fatalist, Komodoflorensal."

As he spoke Tarzan crossed the room and standing at the prince's side took hold of the bars at the window. "They do not seem over-heavy," he remarked, and at the same time exerted pressure upon them. They bent!

Tarzan was interested now and Komodoflorensal, as well. The ape-man threw all his strength and weight into the succeeding effort with the result that two bars, bent almost double, were torn from their setting.

Komodoflorensal gazed at him in astonishment. "Zoanthrohago reduced your size, but left you with your former physical prowess," he cried.

"In no other way can it be accounted for," replied Tarzan, who now, one by one, was removing the remaining bars from the window embrasure. He straightened one of the shorter ones and handed it to Komodoflorensal. "This will make a good weapon," he said, "if we are forced to fight for our liberty," and then he straightened another for himself.

The Trohanadalmakusian gazed at him in wonder. "And you intend," he demanded, "to defy a city of four hundred and eighty thousand people, armed only with a bit of iron rod?"

"And my wits," added Tarzan.

1924

11 ROTWANG

Thea von Harbou

Deploring the inefficiencies of Metropolis's laborers, Joh Fredersen, master of this futuristic dystopian city-state, envisions a technological fix. Although he and Rotwang, a superlatively gifted scientist who lives and works in a wizard's eerie dwelling, were formerly rivals for the love of the same woman, Fredersen has persuaded his frenemy to develop *maschinenmenschen*—that is, mechanical workers. In the *Metropolis* scene excerpted here, Fredersen checks up on Rotwang's progress in this diabolical experiment.

* * *

There were in Metropolis, in this city of reasoned, methodical hurry, very many who would rather have gone far out of their way than have passed by Rotwang's house. It hardly reached knee-high to the house-giants which stood near it. It stood at an angle to the street. To the cleanly town, which knew neither smoke nor soot, it was a blot and an annoyance. But it remained. When Rotwang left the house and crossed the street, which occurred but seldom, there were many who covertly looked at his feet, to see if, perhaps, he walked in red shoes.

Before the door of this house, on which the seal of Solomon glowed, stood Joh Fredersen.

He had sent the car away and had knocked.

He waited, then knocked again.

A voice asked, as if the house were speaking in its sleep: "Who is there?"

"Joh Fredersen," said the man.

The door opened.

He entered. The door closed. He stood in darkness. But Joh Fredersen knew the house well. He walked straight on, and as he walked, the shimmering tracks of two stepping feet glistened before him, along the passage, and the edge of the stair began to glow. Like a dog showing the track, the glow ran on before him, up the steps, to die out behind him.

He reached the top of the stairs and looked about him. He knew that many doors opened out here. But on the one opposite him the copper seal glowed like a distorted eye, which looked at him.

He stepped up to it. The door opened before him.

Many doors as Rotwang's house possessed, this was the only one which opened itself to Joh Fredersen, although, and even, perhaps, because, the owner of this house knew full well that it always meant no mean effort for Joh Fredersen to cross this threshold.

He drew in the air of the room, lingeringly, but deeply, as though seeking in it the trace of another breath . . .

His nonchalant hand threw his hat on a chair. Slowly, in sudden and mournful weariness, he let his eyes wander through the room.

It was almost empty. A large, time-blackened chair, such as are to be found in old churches, stood before drawn curtains. These curtains covered a recess the width of the wall.

Joh Fredersen remained standing by the door for a long time, without moving. He had closed his eyes. With incomparable impotence he breathed in the odour of hyacinths, which teemed to fill the motionless air of this room.

Without opening his eyes, swaying a little, but aim-sure, he walked up to the heavy, black curtains and drew them apart.

Then he opened his eyes and stood quite still . . .

On a pedestal, the breadth of the wall, rested the head of a woman in stone . . .

It was not the work of an artist, it was the work of a man, who, in agonies for which the human tongue lacks words, had wrestled with the white stone throughout immeasurable days and nights until at last it seemed to realise and form the woman's head by itself. It was as if no tool had been at work here—no, it was as if a man, lying before this stone, had called on the name of the woman, unceasingly, with all the strength, with all the longing, with all the despair, of his brain, blood and heart, until the shapeless stone took pity on him letting itself turn into the image of the woman, who had meant to two men all heaven and all hell.

Joh Fredersen's eyes sank to the words which were hewn into the pedestal, roughly, as though chiselled with curses.

HEL

BORN

TO BE MY HAPPINESS, A BLESSING TO ALL MEN

LOST

TO JOH FREDERSEN

DYING IN GIVING LIFE TO HIS SON, FREDER

Yes, she died then. But Joh Fredersen knew only too well that she did not die from giving birth to her child. She died then because she had done what she had to do. She really died on the day upon which she went from Rotwang to Joh Fredersen, wondering that her feet left no bloody traces behind on the way. She had died because she was unable to withstand the great love of Joh Fredersen and because she had been forced by him to tear asunder the life of another.

Never was the expression of deliverance at last more strong upon a human face than upon Hel's face when she knew that she would die.

But in the same hour the mightiest man in Metropolis had lain on the floor, screaming like a wild beast, the bones of which are being broken in its living body.

And, on his meeting Rotwang, four weeks later, he found that the dense, disordered hair over the wonderful brow of the inventor was snow-white, and in the eyes under this brow the smouldering of a hatred which was very closely related to madness.

In this great love, in this great hatred, the poor, dead Hel had remained alive to both men . . .

"You must wait a little while," said the voice which sounded as though the house were talking in its sleep.

"Listen, Rotwang," said Joh Fredersen. "You know that I treat your little juggling tricks with patience, and that I come to you when I want anything of you, and that you are the only man who can say that of himself. But you will never get me to join in with you when you play the fool. You know, too, that I have no time to waste. Don't make us both ridiculous, but come!"

"I told you that you would have to wait a little while," explained the voice, seeming to grow more distant.

"I shall not wait. I shall go."

"Do so, Joh Fredersen!"

He wanted to do so. But the door through which he had entered had no key, no latch. The seal of Solomon, glowing copper-red, blinked at him.

A soft, far-off voice laughed.

Joh Fredersen had stopped still, his back to the room. A quiver ran down his back, running along the hanging arms to the clenched fists.

"You should have your skull smashed in," said Joh Fredersen, very softly. "You should have your skull smashed in . . . that is, if it did not contain so valuable a brain . . ."

"You can do no more to me than you have done," said the far-off voice.

Joh Fredersen was silent.

"Which do you think," continued the voice, "to be more painful: to smash in the skull, or to tear the heart out of the body?"

Joh Fredersen was silent.

"Are your wits frozen, that you don't answer, Joh Fredersen?"

"A brain like yours should be able to forget," said the man standing at the door, staring at Solomon's seal.

The soft, far-off voice laughed.

"Forget? I have twice in my life forgotten something . . . Once that Aetro-oil and quicksilver have an idiosyncrasy as regards each other; that cost me my arm. Secondly that Hel was a woman and you a man; that cost me my heart. The third time, I am afraid, it will cost me my head. I shall never again forget anything, Joh Fredersen."

Joh Fredersen was silent.

The far-off voice was silent, too.

Joh Fredersen turned round and walked to the table. He piled books and parchments on top of each other, sat down and took a piece of paper from his pocket. He laid it before him and looked at it.

It was no larger than a man's hand, bearing neither print nor script, being covered over and over with the tracing of a strange symbol and an apparently half-destroyed plan. Ways seemed to be indicated, seeming to be false ways, but they all led one way; to a place that was filled with crosses.

Suddenly he felt, from the back, a certain coldness approaching him. Involuntarily he held his breath.

A hand grasped along, by his head, a graceful, skeleton hand. Transparent skin was stretched over the slender joints, which gleamed beneath it like dull silver. Fingers, snow-white and fleshless, closed over the plan which lay on the table, and, lifting it up, took it away with it.

Joh Fredersen swung around. He stared at the being which stood before him with eyes which grew glassy.

The being was, indubitably, a woman. In the soft garment which it wore stood a body, like the body of a young birch tree, swaying on feet set fast together. But, although it was a woman, it was not human. The body seemed as though made of crystal, through which the bones shone silver. Cold streamed from the glazen skin which did not contain a drop of blood. The being held its beautiful hands pressed against its breast, which was motionless, with a gesture of determination, almost of defiance.

But the being had no face. The beautiful curve of the neck bore a lump of carelessly shaped mass. The skull was bald, nose, lips, temples merely traced. Eyes, as though painted on closed lids, stared unseeingly, with an expression of calm madness, at the man—who did not breathe.

"Be courteous, my parody," said the far-off voice, which sounded as though the house were talking in its sleep. "Greet Joh Fredersen, the Master over the great Metropolis."

The being bowed slowly to the man. The mad eyes neared him like two darting flames. The mass began to speak; it said in a voice full of a horrible tenderness: "Good evening, Joh Fredersen."

And these words were more alluring than a half-open mouth.

"Good, my Pearl! Good, my Crown-jewel!" said the far-off voice, full of praise and pride.

But at the same moment the being lost its balance. It fell, tipping forward, towards Joh Fredersen. He stretched out his hands to catch it, feeling them, in the moment of contact, to be burnt by an unbearable coldness, the brutality of which brought up in him a feeling of anger and disgust.

He pushed the being away from him and towards Rotwang, who was standing near him as though fallen from the air. Rotwang took the being by the arm.

He shook his head. "Too violent," he said. "Too violent. My beautiful parody, I fear your temperament will get you into much more trouble."

"What is that?" asked Joh Fredersen, leaning his hands against the edge of the table-top, which he felt behind him.

Rotwang turned his face towards him, his glorious eyes glowing as watch fires glow when the wind lashes them with its cold lash.

"Who is it?" he replied. "Futura . . . Parody . . . whatever you like to call it. Also: delusion . . . In short: It is a woman . . . Every man-creator makes himself a woman. I do not believe that humbug about the first human being a man. If a male-god created the world (which is to be hoped, Joh Fredersen) then he certainly created woman first, lovingly and revelling in creative sport. You can test it, Joh Fredersen: it is faultless. A little cool—I admit, that comes of the material, which is my secret. But she is not yet completely finished. She is not yet discharged from the workshop of her creator. I cannot make up my mind to do it. You understand that? Completion means setting free. I do not want to set her free from me. That is why I have not yet given her a face. You must give her that, Joh Fredersen. For you were the one to order the new beings."

"I ordered machine men from you, Rotwang, which I can use at my machines. No woman . . . no plaything."

"No plaything, Joh Fredersen, no . . . you and I, we no longer play. Not for any stakes . . . We did it once. Once and never again. No plaything, Joh Fredersen but a tool. Do you know what it means to have a woman as a tool?

A woman like this, faultless and cool? And obedient—
implicitly obedient . . . Why do you fight with the Goth-
ics and the monk Desertus about the cathedral? Send the
woman to them Joh Fredersen! Send the woman to them
when they are kneeling, scourging themselves. Let this
faultless, cool woman walk through the rows of them, on
her silver feet, fragrance from the garden of life in the
folds of her garment . . . Who in the world knows how the
blossoms of the tree smell, on which the apple of knowledge ripened. The woman is both: Fragrance of the blos-
som and the fruit . . .

"Shall I explain to you the newest creation of Rotwang,
the genius, Joh Fredersen? It will be sacrilege. But I owe
it to you. For you kindled the idea of creating within me,
too . . . Shall I show you how obedient my creature is?
Give me what you have in your hand, Parody!"

"Stop . . ." said Joh Fredersen rather hoarsely. But the
infallible obedience of the creature which stood before
the two men brooked no delay in obeying. It opened its
hands in which the delicate bones shimmered silver, and
handed to its creator the piece of paper which it had taken
from the table, before Joh Fredersen's eyes.

"That's trickery, Rotwang," said Joh Fredersen.

The great inventor looked at him. He laughed. The
noiseless laughter drew back his mouth to his ears.

"No trickery, Joh Fredersen—the work of a genius! Shall
Futura dance to you? Shall my beautiful Parody play the
affectionate? Or the sulky? Cleopatra of Damayanti? Shall
she have the gestures of the Gothic Madonnas? Or the
gestures of love of an Asiatic dancer? What hair shall I

plant upon the skull of your tool? Shall she be modest or impudent? Excuse me my many words, you man of few! I am drunk, d'you see, drunk with being a creator. I intoxicate myself, I inebriate myself, on your astonished face! I have surpassed your expectations, Joh Fredersen, haven't I? And you do not know everything yet: my beautiful Parody can sing, too! She can also read! The mechanism of her brain is as infallible as that of your own, Joh Fredersen!"

"If that is so," said the Master over the great Metropolis, with a certain dryness in his voice, which had become quite hoarse, "then command her to unriddle the plan which you have in your hand, Rotwang . . ."

Rotwang burst out into laughter which was like the laughter of a drunken man. He threw a glance at the piece of paper which he held spread out in his fingers, and was about to pass it, anticipatingly triumphant, to the being which stood beside him.

But he stopped in the middle of the movement. With open mouth, he stared at the piece of paper, raising it nearer and nearer to his eyes.

Joh Fredersen, who was watching him, bent forward. He wanted to say something, to ask a question. But before he could open his lips Rotwang threw up his head and met Joh Fredersen's glance with so green a fire in his eyes that the Master of the great Metropolis remained dumb.

Twice, three times did this green glow flash between the piece of paper and Joh Fredersen's face. And during the whole time not a sound was perceptible in the room but the breath that gushed in heaves from Rotwang's breast as though from a boiling, poisoned source.

"Where did you get the plan?" the great inventor asked at last. Though it was less a question than an expression of astonished anger.

"That is not the point," answered Joh Fredersen. "It is about this that I have come to you. There does not seem to be a soul in Metropolis who can make anything of it."

Rotwang's laughter interrupted him.

"Your poor scholars!" cried the laugher. "What a task you have set them, Joh Fredersen. How many hundredweights of printed paper have you forced them to heave over. I am sure there is no town on the globe, from the construction of the old Tower of Babel onward, which they have not snuffled through from North to South. Oh— If you could only smile, Parody! If only you already had eyes to wink at me. But laugh, at least, Parody! Laugh, ripplingly, at the great scholars to whom the ground under their feet is foreign!"

The being obeyed. It laughed, ripplingly.

"Then you know the plan, or what it represents?" asked Joh Fredersen, through the laughter.

"Yes, by my poor soul, I know it," answered Rotwang. "But, by my poor soul, I am not going to tell you what it is until you tell me where you got the plan."

Joh Fredersen reflected. Rotwang did not take his gaze from him. "Do not try to lie to me, Joh Fredersen," he said softly, and with a whimsical melancholy.

"Somebody found the paper," began Joh Fredersen.

"Who—somebody?"

"One of my foremen."

"Grot?"

"Yes, Grot."

"Where did he find the plan?"

"In the pocket of a workman who was killed in the accident to the Geyser machine."

"Grot brought you the paper?"

"Yes."

"And the meaning of the plan seemed to be unknown to him?"

Joh Fredersen hesitated a moment with the answer. "The meaning—yes; but not the plan. He told me he has often seen this paper in the workmen's hands, and that they anxiously keep it a secret, and that the men will crowd closely around him who holds it."

"So the meaning of the plan has been kept secret from your foreman."

"So it seems, for he could not explain it to me."

"H'm."

Rotwang turned to the being which was standing near him, with the appearance of listening intently.

"What do you say about it, my beautiful Parody?"

The being stood motionless.

"Well—?" said Joh Fredersen, with a sharp expression of impatience. Rotwang looked at him, jerkily turning his great skull towards him. The glorious eyes crept behind their lids as though wishing to have nothing in common with the strong white teeth and the jaws of the beast of prey. But from beneath the almost closed lids they gazed at Joh Fredersen, as though they sought in his face the door to the great brain.

"How can one bind you, Joh Fredersen," he murmured, "what is a word to you—or an oath . . . Oh God . . . you with your own laws. What promise would you keep if the breaking of it seemed expedient to you?"

"Don't talk rubbish, Rotwang," said Joh Fredersen. "I shall hold my tongue because I still need you. I know quite well that the people whom we need are our solitary tyrants. So, if you know, speak."

Rotwang still hesitated; but gradually a smile took possession of his features—a good natured and mysterious smile, which was amusing itself at itself.

"You are standing on the entrance," he said.

"What does that mean?"

"To be taken literally, Joh Fredersen! You are standing on the entrance."

"What entrance, Rotwang? You are wasting time that does not belong to you . . ."

The smile on Rotwang's face deepened to serenity.

"Do you recollect, Joh Fredersen, how obstinately I refused, that time, to let the underground railway be run under my house?"

"Indeed I do! I still know the sum the detour cost me, also!"

"The secret was expensive, I admit, but it was worth it. Just take a look at the plan, Joh Fredersen, what is that?"

"Perhaps a flight of stairs . . ."

"Quite certainly a flight of stairs. It is a very slovenly execution in the drawing as in reality . . ."

"So you know them?"

"I have the honour, Joh Fredersen—yes. Now come two paces sideways. What is that?"

He had taken Joh Fredersen by the arm. He felt the fingers of the artificial hand pressing into his muscles like the claws of a bird of prey. With the right one Rotwang indicated the spot upon which Joh Fredersen had stood.

"What is that?" he asked, shaking the hand which he held in his grip.

Joh Fredersen bent down. He straightened himself up again. "A door?"

"Right, Joh Fredersen! A door! A perfectly fitting and well shutting door. The man who built this house was an orderly and careful person. Only once did he omit to give heed, and then he had to pay for it. He went down the stairs which are under the door, followed the careless steps and passages which are connected with them, and never found his way back. It is not easy to find, for those who lodged there did not care to have strangers penetrate into their domain . . . I found my inquisitive predecessor, Joh Fredersen, and recognised him at once—by his pointed red shoes, which have preserved themselves wonderfully. As a corpse he looked peaceful and Christian—like, both of which he certainly was not in his life. The companions of his last hours probably contributed considerably to the conversion of the erstwhile devil's disciple . . ."

He tapped with his right forefinger upon a maze of crosses in the centre of the plan.

"Here he lies. Just on this spot. His skull must have enclosed a brain which was worthy of your own, Joh Fredersen, and he had to perish because he once lost his way... What a pity for him..."

"Where did he lose his way?" asked Joh Fredersen.

Rotwang looked long at him before speaking. "In the city of graves, over which Metropolis stands," he answered at last. "Deep below the moles' tunnels of your underground railway, Joh Fredersen, lies the thousand-year-old Metropolis of the thousand-year-old dead..."

Joh Fredersen was silent. His left eyebrow rose, while his eyes narrowed. He fixed his gaze upon Rotwang, who had not taken his eyes from him.

"What is the plan of this city of graves doing in the hands and pockets of my workmen?"

"That is yet to be discovered," answered Rotwang.

"Will you help me?"

"Yes."

"Tonight?"

"Very well."

"I shall come back after the changing of the shift."

"Do so, Joh Fredersen. And if you take some good advice..."

"Well?"

"Come in the uniform of your workmen, when you come back!"

Joh Fredersen raised his head but the great inventor did not let him speak. He raised his hand as one calling for and admonishing to silence.

"The skull of the man in the red shoes also enclosed a powerful brain, Joh Fredersen, but nevertheless, he could not find his way homewards from those who dwell down there..."

Joh Fredersen reflected. He nodded and turned to go.

"Be courteous, my beautiful Parody," said Rotwang. "Open the doors for the Master over the great Metropolis."

The being glided past Joh Fredersen. He felt the breath of coldness which came forth from it. He saw the silent laughter between the half-open lips of Rotwang, the great inventor. He turned pale with rage, but he remained silent.

The being stretched out the transparent hand in which the bones shone silver, and, touching it with its fingertips, moved the seal of Solomon, which glowed copperish.

The door yielded back. Joh Fredersen went out after the being, which stepped downstairs before him.

There was no light on the stairs, nor in the narrow passage. But a shimmer came from the being no stronger than that of a green-burning candle, yet strong enough to lighten up the stairs and the black walls.

At the house-door the being stopped still and waited for Joh Fredersen, who was walking slowly along behind it. The house-door opened before him, but not far enough for him to pass out through the opening.

The eyes stared at him from the mass-head of the being, eyes as though painted on closed lids, with the expression of calm madness.

"Be courteous, my beautiful Parody," said a soft, far-off voice, which sounded as though the house were talking in its sleep.

The being bowed. It stretched out a hand—a graceful skeleton hand. Transparent skin was stretched over the slender joints, which gleamed beneath it like dull silver. Fingers, snow-white and fleshless, opened like the petals of a crystal lily.

Joh Fredersen laid his hand in it, feeling it, in the moment of contact, to be burnt by an unbearable coldness. He wanted to push the being away from him but the silver-crystal fingers held him fast.

"Good-bye, Joh Fredersen," said the mass head, in a voice full of a horrible tenderness. "Give me a face soon, Joh Fredersen!"

A soft far-off voice laughed, as if the house were laughing in its sleep.

The hand left go, the door opened, Joh Fredersen reeled into the street.

1925

12 PROFESSOR CHALLENGER
Arthur Conan Doyle

In the penultimate Professor Challenger adventure, Doyle's superman—"a primitive cave-man in a lounge suit," one hears, while simultaneously "the greatest brain in Europe"—sets about drilling his way to a point eight miles beneath our planet's epidermis. Why? In order to test the bold hypothesis that the Earth is a sentient organism! Presented in its entirety here, the story needs no contextualizing . . . except, perhaps, to note that Edward Malone is Challenger's comrade from previous adventures.

* * *

I had a vague recollection of having heard my friend Edward Malone, of the *Gazette*, speak of Professor Challenger, with whom he had been associated in some remarkable adventures. I am so busy, however, with my own profession, and my firm has been so overtaxed with orders, that I know little of what is going on in the world outside my own special interests. My general recollection was that Challenger has been depicted as a wild genius of a violent and intolerant disposition. I was greatly surprised to receive a business communication from him which was in the following terms:

14 (Bis),
Enmore Gardens,
Kensington.

Sir,—

I have occasion to engage the services of an expert in Artesian borings. I will not conceal from you that my opinion of experts is not a high one, and that I have usually found that a man who, like myself, has a well-equipped brain can take a sounder and broader view than the man who professes a special knowledge (which, alas, is so often a mere profession), and is therefore limited in his outlook. None the less, I am disposed to give you a trial. Looking down the list of Artesian authorities, a certain oddity—I had almost written absurdity—in your name attracted my attention, and I found upon inquiry that my young friend, Mr. Edward Malone, was actually acquainted with you. I am therefore writing to say that I should be glad to have an interview with you, and that if you satisfy my requirements, and my standard is no mean one, I may be inclined to put a most important matter into your hands. I can say no more at present as the matter is of extreme secrecy, which can only be discussed by word of mouth. I beg, therefore, that you will at once cancel any engagement which you may happen to have, and that you will call upon me at the above address at 10:30 in the morning of next Friday. There is a scraper as well as a mat, and Mrs. Challenger is most particular.

               I remain, Sir, as I began,

               George Edward Challenger.

I handed this letter to my chief clerk to answer, and he informed the Professor that Mr. Peerless Jones would be glad to keep the appointment as arranged. It was a perfectly civil business note, but it began with the phrase: "Your letter (undated) has been received."

This drew a second epistle from the Professor: "Sir," he said, and his writing looked like a barbed wire fence—

> I observe that you animadvert upon the trifle that my letter was undated. Might I draw your attention to the fact that, as some return for a monstrous taxation, our Government is in the habit of affixing a small circular sign or stamp upon the outside on the envelope which notifies the date of posting? Should this sign be missing or illegible your remedy lies with the proper postal authorities. Meanwhile, I would ask you to confine your observations to matters which concern the business over which I consult you, and to cease to comment upon the form which my own letters may assume.

It was clear to me that I was dealing with a lunatic, so I thought it well before I went any further in the matter to call upon my friend Malone, whom I had known since the old days when we both played Rugger for Richmond. I found him the same jolly Irishman as ever, and much amused at my first brush with Challenger.

"That's nothing, my boy," said he. "You'll feel as if you had been skinned alive when you have been with him five minutes. He beats the world for offensiveness."

"But why should the world put up with it?"

"They don't. If you collected all the libel actions and all the rows and all the police-court assaults—"

"Assaults!"

"Bless you, he would think nothing of throwing you downstairs if you have a disagreement. He is a primitive cave-man in a lounge suit. I can see him with a club in one hand and a jagged bit of flint in the other. Some people are born out of their proper century, but he is born out of his millennium. He belongs to the early neolithic or thereabouts."

"And he a professor!"

"There is the wonder of it! It's the greatest brain in Europe, with a driving force behind it that can turn all his dreams into facts. They do all they can to hold him back for his colleagues hate him like poison, but a lot of trawlers might as well try to hold back the *Berengaria*. He simply ignores them and steams on his way."

"Well," said I, "one thing is clear. I don't want to have anything to do with him. I'll cancel that appointment."

"Not a bit of it. You will keep it to the minute—and mind that it is to the minute or you will hear of it."

"Why should I?"

"Well, I'll tell you. First of all, don't take too seriously what I have said about old Challenger. Everyone who gets close to him learns to love him. There is no real harm in the old bear. Why, I remember how he carried an Indian baby with the smallpox on his back for a hundred miles from the back country down to the Madeira river. He is big in every way. He won't hurt if you get right with him."

"I won't give him the chance."

"You will be a fool if you don't. Have you ever heard of the Hengist Down Mystery—the shaft-sinking on the South Coast?"

"Some secret coal-mining exploration, I understand."

Malone winked.

"Well, you can put it down as that if you like. You see, I am in the old man's confidence, and I can't say anything until he gives the word. But I may tell you this, for it has been in the Press. A man, Betterton, who made his money in rubber, left his whole estate to Challenger some years ago, with the provision that it should be used in the interests of science. It proved to be an enormous sum—several millions. Challenger then bought a property at Hengist Down, in Sussex. It was worthless land on the north edge of the chalk country, and he got a large tract of it, which he wired off. There was a deep gully in the middle of it. Here he began to make an excavation. He announced"—here Malone winked again—"that there was petroleum in England and that he meant to prove it. He built a little model village with a colony of well-paid workers who are all sworn to keep their mouths shut. The gully is wired off as well as the estate, and the place is guarded by bloodhounds. Several pressmen have nearly lost their lives, to say nothing of the seats of their trousers, from these creatures. It's a big operation, and Sir Thomas Morden's firm has it in hand, but they also are sworn to secrecy. Clearly the time has come when Artesian help is needed. Now, would you not be foolish to refuse such a job as that, with all the interest and experience and a big fat cheque at the end of it—to say nothing of rubbing shoulders with the most wonderful man you have ever met or are ever likely to meet?"

Malone's arguments prevailed, and Friday morning found me on my way to Enmore Gardens. I took such particular care to be on time that I found myself at the door twenty minutes too soon. I was waiting in the street when it struck me that I recognized the Rolls-Royce with the silver arrow mascot at the door. It was certainly that of

Jack Devonshire, the junior partner of the great Morden firm. I had always known him as the most urbane of men, so that it was rather a shock to me when he suddenly appeared, and standing outside the door he raised both his hands, to heaven and said with great fervour: "Damn him! Oh, damn him!"

"What is up, Jack? You seem peeved this morning."

"Hullo, Peerless! Are you in on this job, too?"

"There seems a chance of it."

"Well, you'll find it chastening to the temper."

"Rather more so than yours can stand, apparently."

"Well, I should say so. The butler's message to me was: 'The Professor desired me to say, sir, that he was rather busy at present eating an egg, and that if you would call at some more convenient time he would very likely see you.' That was the message delivered by a servant. I may add that I had called to collect forty-two thousand pounds that he owes us."

I whistled.

"You can't get your money?"

"Oh, yes, he is all right about money. I'll do the old gorilla the justice to say that he is open-handed with money. But he pays when he likes and how he likes, and he cares for nobody. However, you go and try your luck and see how you like it." With that he flung himself into his motor and was off.

I waited with occasional glances at my watch until the zero hour should arrive. I am, if I may say so, a fairly hefty individual, and a runner-up for the Belsize Boxing Club middle-weights, but I have never faced an interview with such trepidation as this. It was not physical, for I was confident I could hold my own if this inspired lunatic should attack me, but it was a mixture of feelings in which fear of some public scandal and dread of losing a lucrative contract were mingled. However, things are always easier when imagination ceases and action begins. I snapped up my watch and made for the door.

It was opened by an old wooden-faced butler, a man who bore an expression, or an absence of expression, which gave the impression that he was so inured to shocks that nothing on earth would surprise him.

"By appointment, sir?" he asked.

"Certainly."

He glanced at a list in his hand.

"Your name, sir? . . . Quite so, Mr. Peerless Jones. . . . Ten-thirty. Everything is in order. We have to be careful, Mr. Jones, for we are much annoyed by journalists. The Professor, as you may be aware, does not approve of the Press. This way, sir. Professor Challenger is now receiving."

The next instant I found myself in the presence. I believe that my friend, Ted Malone, has described the man in his "Lost World" yarn better than I can hope to do, so I'll leave it at that. All I was aware of was a huge trunk of a man behind a mahogany desk, with a great spade-shaped black beard and two large grey eyes half covered with insolent drooping eyelids. His big head sloped back, his beard bristled forward, and his whole appearance conveyed one single impression of arrogant intolerance. "Well, what the devil do you want?" was written all over him. I laid my card on the table.

"Ah yes," he said, picking it up and handling it as if he disliked the smell of it. "Of course. You are the expert so-called. Mr. Jones—Mr. Peerless Jones. You may thank your godfather, Mr. Jones, for it was this ludicrous prefix which first drew my attention to you."

"I am here, Professor Challenger, for a business interview and not to discuss my own name," said I, with all the dignity I could master.

"Dear me, you seem to be a very touchy person, Mr. Jones. Your nerves are in a highly irritable condition. We must walk warily in dealing with you, Mr. Jones. Pray sit down and compose yourself. I have been reading your little brochure upon the reclaiming of the Sinai Peninsula. Did you write it yourself?"

"Naturally, sir. My name is on it."

"Quite so! Quite so! But it does not always follow, does it? However, I am prepared to accept your assertion. The book is not without merit of a sort. Beneath the dullness of the diction one gets glimpses of an occasional idea. There are germs of thought here and there. Are you a married man?"

"No, sir. I am not."

"Then there is some chance of your keeping a secret."

"If I promised to do so, I would certainly keep my promise."

"So you say. My young friend, Malone"—he spoke as if Ted were ten years of age—"has a good opinion of you. He says that I may trust you. This trust is a very great one, for I am engaged just now in one of the greatest experiments—I may even say the greatest experiment—in the history of the world. I ask for your participation."

"I shall be honoured."

"It is indeed an honour. I will admit that I should have shared my labours with no one were it not that the gigantic nature of the undertaking calls for the highest technical skill. Now, Mr. Jones, having obtained your promise of inviolable secrecy, I come down to the essential point. It is this—that the world upon which we live is itself a living organism, endowed, as I believe, with a circulation, a respiration, and a nervous system of its own."

Clearly the man was a lunatic.

"Your brain, I observe," he continued, "fails to register. But it will gradually absorb the idea. You will recall how a moor or heath resembles the hairy side of a giant animal. A certain analogy runs through all nature. You will then consider the secular rise and fall of land, which indicates the slow respiration of the creature. Finally, you will note the fidgetings and scratchings which appear to our Lilliputian perceptions as earthquakes and convulsions."

"What about volcanoes?" I asked.

"Tut, tut! They correspond to the heat spots upon our own bodies."

My brain whirled as I tried to find some answer to these monstrous contentions.

"The temperature!" I cried. "Is it not a fact that it rises rapidly as one descends, and that the centre of the earth is liquid heat?"

He waved my assertion aside.

"You are probably aware, sir, since Council schools are now compulsory, that the earth is flattened at the poles. This means that the pole is nearer to the centre than any other point and would therefore be most affected by this heat of which you spoke. It is notorious, of course, that the conditions of the poles are tropical, is it not?"

"The whole idea is utterly new to me."

"Of course it is. It is the privilege of the original thinker to put forward ideas which are new and usually unwelcome to the common clay. Now, sir, what is this?" He held up a small object which he had picked from the table.

"I should say it is a sea-urchin."

"Exactly!" he cried, with an air of exaggerated surprise, as when an infant has done something clever. "It is a sea-urchin—a common echinus. Nature repeats itself in many forms regardless of the size. This echinus is a model, a prototype, of the world. You perceive that it is roughly circular, but flattened at the poles. Let us then regard the world as a huge echinus. What are your objections?"

My chief objection was that the thing was too absurd for argument, but I did not dare to say so. I fished around for some less sweeping assertion.

"A living creature needs food," I said. "Where could the world sustain its huge bulk?"

"An excellent point—excellent!" said the Professor, with a huge air of patronage. "You have a quick eye for the obvious, though you are slow in realizing the more subtle implications. How does the world get nourishment? Again we turn to our little friend the echinus. The water which surrounds it flows through the tubes of this small creature and provides its nutrition."

"Then you think that the water—"

"No, sir. The ether. The earth browses upon a circular path in the fields of space, and as it moves the ether is continually pouring through it and providing its vitality. Quite a flock of other little world-echini are doing the same thing, Venus, Mars, and the rest, each with its own field for grazing."

The man was clearly mad, but there was no arguing with him. He accepted my silence as agreement and smiled at me in a most beneficent fashion.

"We are coming on, I perceive," said he. "Light is beginning to break in. A little dazzling at first, no doubt, but we will soon get used to it. Pray give me your attention while I found one or two more observations upon this little creature in my hand.

"We will suppose that on this outer hard rind there were certain infinitely small insects which crawled upon the surface. Would the echinus ever be aware of their existence?"

"I should say not."

"You can well imagine then, that the earth has not the least idea of the way in which it is utilized by the human race. It is quite unaware of this fungus growth of vegetation and evolution of tiny animalcules which has collected upon it during its travels round the sun as barnacles gather upon the ancient vessel. That is the present state of affairs, and that is what I propose to alter."

I stared in amazement. "You propose to alter it?"

"I propose to let the earth know that there is at least one person, George Edward Challenger, who calls for attention—who, indeed, insists upon attention. It is certainly the first intimation it has ever had of the sort."

"And how, sir, will you do this?"

"Ah, there we get down to business. You have touched the spot. I will again call your attention to this interesting little creature which I hold in my hand. It is all nerves and sensibility beneath that protective crust. Is it not evident that if a parasitic animalcule desired to call its attention it would sink a hole in its shell and so stimulate its sensory apparatus?"

"Certainly."

"Or, again, we will take the case of the homely flea or a mosquito which explores the surface of the human body. We may be unaware of its presence. But presently, when it sinks its proboscis through the skin, which is our crust, we are disagreeably reminded that we are not altogether alone. My plans now will no doubt begin to dawn upon you. Light breaks in the darkness."

"Good heavens! You propose to sink a shaft through the earth's crust?"

He closed his eyes with ineffable complacency.

"You see before you," he said, "the first who will ever pierce that horny hide. I may even put it in the present tense and say who has pierced it."

"You have done it!"

"With the very efficient aid of Morden, I think I may say that I have done it. Several years of constant work which has been carried on night and day, and conducted by every known species of drill, borer, crusher, and explosive, has at last brought us to our goal."

"You don't mean to say you are through the crust!"

"If your expressions denote bewilderment they may pass. If they denote incredulity—"

"No, sir, nothing of the kind."

"You will accept my statement without question. We are through the crust. It was exactly fourteen thousand four hundred and forty-two yards thick, or roughly eight miles. In the course of our sinking it may interest you to know that we have exposed a fortune in the matter of coal-beds which would probably in the long run defray the cost of the enterprise. Our chief difficulty has been the springs of water in the lower chalk and Hastings sands, but these we have overcome. The last stage has now been reached—and the last stage is none other than Mr. Peerless Jones. You, sir, represent the mosquito. Your Artesian borer takes the place of the stinging proboscis. The brain has done its work. Exit the thinker. Enter the mechanical one, the peerless one, with his rod of metal. Do I make myself clear?"

"You talk of eight miles!" I cried. "Are you aware, sir, that five thousand feet is considered nearly the limit for Artesian borings? I am acquainted with one in upper Silesia which is six thousand two hundred feet deep, but it is looked upon as a wonder."

"You misunderstand me, Mr. Peerless. Either my explanation or your brain is at fault, and I will not insist upon which. I am well aware of the limits of Artesian borings, and it is not likely that I would have spent millions of pounds upon my colossal tunnel if a six-inch boring would have met my needs. All that I ask you is to have a drill ready which shall be as sharp as possible, not more than a hundred feet in length, and operated by an electric motor. An ordinary percussion drill driven home by a weight will meet every requirement."

"Why by an electric motor?"

"I am here, Mr. Jones, to give orders, not reasons. Before we finish it may happen—it may, I say, happen—that your very life may depend upon this drill being started from a distance by electricity. It can, I presume, be done?"

"Certainly it can be done."

"Then prepare to do it. The matter is not yet ready for your actual presence, but your preparations may now be made. I have nothing more to say.'"

"But it is essential," I expostulated, "that you should let me know what soil the drill is to penetrate. Sand, or clay, or chalk would each need different treatment."

"Let us say jelly," said Challenger. "Yes, we will for the present suppose that you have to sink your drill into jelly. And now, Mr. Jones, I have matters of some importance to engage my mind, so I will wish you good morning. You can draw up a formal contract with mention of your charges for my Head of Works."

I bowed and turned, but before I reached the door my curiosity overcame me. He was already writing furiously with a quill pen screeching over the paper, and he looked up angrily at my interruption.

"Well, sir, what now? I had hoped you were gone."

"I only wished to ask you, sir, what the object of so extraordinary an experiment can be?"

"Away, sir, away!" he cried, angrily. "Raise your mind above the base mercantile and utilitarian needs of commerce. Shake off your paltry standards of business. Science seeks knowledge. Let the knowledge lead us where it will, we still must seek it. To know once for all what we are, why we are, where we are, is that not in itself the greatest of all human aspirations? Away, sir, away!"

His great black head was bowed over his papers once more and blended with his beard. The quill pen screeched more shrilly than ever. So I left him, this extraordinary man, with my head in a whirl at the thought of the strange business in which I now found myself to be his partner.

When I got back to my office I found Ted Malone waiting with a broad grin upon his face to know the result of my interview.

"Well!" he cried. "None the worse? No case of assault and battery? You must have handled him very tactfully. What do you think of the old boy?"

"The most aggravating, insolent, intolerant, self-opinionated man I have ever met, but—"

"Exactly!" cried Malone. "We all come to that 'but.' Of course, he is all you say and a lot more, but one feels that so big a man is not to be measured in our scale, and that we can endure from him what we would not stand from any other living mortal. Is that not so?"

"Well, I don't know him well enough yet to say, but I will admit that if he is not a mere bullying megalomaniac, and if what he says is true, then he certainly is in a class by himself. But is it true?"

"Of course it is true. Challenger always delivers the goods. Now, where are you exactly in the matter? Has he told you about Hengist Down?"

"Yes, in a sketchy sort of way."

"Well, you may take it from me that the whole thing is colossal—colossal in conception and colossal in execution.

He hates pressmen, but I am in his confidence, for he knows that I will publish no more than he authorizes. Therefore I have his plans, or some of his plans. He is such a deep old bird that one never is sure if one has really touched bottom. Anyhow, I know enough to assure you that Hengist Down is a practical proposition and nearly completed. My advice to you now is simply to await events, and meanwhile to get your gear all ready. You'll hear soon enough either from him or from me."

As it happened, it was from Malone himself that I heard. He came round quite early to my office some weeks later, as the bearer of a message.

"I've come from Challenger" said he.

"You are like the pilot fish to the shark."

"I'm proud to be anything to him. He really is a wonder. He has done it all right. It's your turn now, and then he is ready to ring up the curtain."

"Well, I can't believe it until I see it, but I have everything ready and loaded on a lorry. I could start it off at any moment."

"Then do so at once. I've given you a tremendous character for energy and punctuality, so mind you don't let me down. In the meantime, come down with me by rail and I will give you an idea of what has to be done."

It was a lovely spring morning—May 22nd, to be exact—when we made that fateful journey which brought me on to a stage which is destined to be historical. On the way Malone handed me a note from Challenger which I was to accept as my instructions.

Sir, (it ran)—

Upon arriving at Hengist Down you will put yourself at the disposal of Mr. Barforth, the Chief Engineer, who is in possession of my plans. My young friend, Malone, the bearer of this, is also in touch with me and may protect me from any personal contact. We have now experienced certain phenomena in the shaft at and below the fourteen thousand-foot level which fully bear out my views as to the nature of a planetary body, but some more sensational proof is needed before I can hope to make an impression upon the torpid intelligence of the modern scientific world. That proof you are destined to afford, and they to witness. As you descend in the lifts you will observe, presuming that you have the rare quality of observation, that you pass in succession the secondary chalk beds, the coal measures, some Devonian and Cambrian indications, and finally the granite, through which the greater part of our tunnel is conducted. The bottom is now covered with tarpaulin, which I order you not to tamper with, as any clumsy handling of the sensitive inner cuticle of the earth might bring about premature results. At my instruction, two strong beams have been laid across the shaft twenty feet above the bottom, with a space between them. This space will act as a clip to hold up your Artesian tube. Fifty feet of drill will suffice, twenty of which will project below the beams, so that the point of the drill comes nearly down to the tarpaulin. As you value your life do not let it go further. Thirty feet will then project upwards in the shaft, and when you have released it we may assume that not less than forty feet of drill will bury itself in the earth's substance. As this substance is very soft I find that you will probably need no driving power, and that simply a release of the tube will suffice by its own weight to drive it into the layer which we have uncovered. These instructions would seem to be sufficient for any ordinary intelligence, but I have little doubt that you will need more, which can be referred to me through our young friend, Malone.

GEORGE EDWARD CHALLENGER.

It can be imagined that when we arrived at the station of Storrington, near the northern foot of the South Downs, I was in a state of considerable nervous tension. A weather-worn Vauxhall thirty landaulette was awaiting us, and bumped us for six or seven miles over by-paths and lanes which, in spite of their natural seclusion, were deeply rutted and showed every sign of heavy traffic. A broken lorry lying in the grass at one point showed that others had found it rough going as well as we. Once a huge piece of machinery which seemed to be the valves and piston of a hydraulic pump projected itself, all rusted, from a clump of furze.

"That's Challenger's doing," said Malone, grinning. "Said it was one-tenth of an inch out of estimate, so he simply chucked it by the wayside."

"With a lawsuit to follow, no doubt."

"A lawsuit! My dear chap, we should have a court of our own. We have enough to keep a judge busy for a year. Government too. The old devil cares for no one. Rex *v*. George Challenger and George Challenger *v*. Rex. A nice devil's dance the two will have from one court to another. Well, here we are. All right, Jenkins, you can let us in!"

A huge man with a notable cauliflower ear was peering into the car, a scowl of suspicion upon his face. He relaxed and saluted as he recognized my companion.

"All right, Mr. Malone. I thought it was the American Associated Press."

"Oh, they are on the track, are they?"

"They to-day, and *The Times* yesterday. Oh, they are buzzing round proper. Look at that!" He indicated a distant dot upon the sky-line.

"See that glint! That's the telescope of the *Chicago Daily News*. Yes, they are fair after us now. I've seen 'em in rows, same as the crows, along the Beacon yonder."

"Poor old Press gang!" said Malone, as we entered a gate in a formidable barbed wire fence. "I am one of them myself, and I know how it feels."

At this moment we heard a plaintive bleat behind us of "Malone! Ted Malone!" It came from a fat little man who had just arrived upon a motor-bike and was at present struggling in the Herculean grasp of the gatekeeper.

"Here, let me go!" he sputtered. "Keep your hands off! Malone, call off this gorilla of yours."

"Let him go, Jenkins! He's a friend of mine!" cried Malone. "Well, old bean, what is it? What are you after in these parts? Fleet Street is your stamping ground—not the wilds of Sussex."

"You know what I am after perfectly well," said our visitor. "I've got the assignment to write a story about Hengist Down and I can't go home without the copy."

"Sorry, Roy, but you can't get anything here. You'll have to stay on that side of the wire. If you want more you must go and see Professor Challenger and get his leave."

"I've been," said the journalist, ruefully. "I went this morning."

"Well, what did he say?"

"He said he would put me through the window."

Malone laughed. "And what did you say?"

"I said, 'What's wrong with the door?' and I skipped through it just to show there was nothing wrong with it. It was no time for argument. I just went. What with that bearded Assyrian bull in London, and this Thug down here, who has ruined my clean celluloid, you seem to be keeping queer company, Ted Malone."

"I can't help you, Roy; I would if I could. They say in Fleet Street that you have never been beaten, but you are up against it this time. Get back to the office, and if you just wait a few days I'll give you the news as soon as the old man allows."

"No chance of getting in?"

"Not an earthly."

"Money no object?"

"You should know better than to say that."

"They tell me it's a shortcut to New Zealand."

"It will be a short cut to the hospital if you butt in here, Roy. Good-bye, now. We have some work to do of our own."

"That's Roy Perkins, the war correspondent," said Malone as we walked across the compound. "We've broken his record, for he is supposed to be undefeatable. It's his fat, little innocent face that carries him through everything. We were on the same staff once. Now there"—he pointed to a cluster of pleasant red-roofed bungalows—"are the quarters of the men. They are a splendid lot of picked workers who are paid far above ordinary rates. They have to be bachelors and teetotallers, and under oath of secrecy. I don't think there has been any leakage up to now. That field is their football ground and the detached house is their library and recreation room. The old man is some organizer, I can assure you. This is Mr. Barforth, the head engineer-in-charge."

A long, thin, melancholy man with deep lines of anxiety upon his face had appeared before us. "I expect you are the Artesian engineer," said he, in a gloomy voice. "I was told to expect you. I am glad you've come, for I don't mind telling you that the responsibility of this thing is getting on my nerves. We work away, and I never know if it's a gush of chalk water, or a seam of coal, or a squirt of petroleum, or maybe a touch of hell fire that is coming next. We've been spared the last up to now, but you may make the connection for all I know."

"Is it so hot down there?"

"Well, it's hot. There's no denying it. And yet maybe it is not hotter than the barometric pressure and the confined space might account for. Of course, the ventilation is awful. We pump the air down, but two-hour shifts are the most the men can do—and they are willing lads too. The Professor was down yesterday, and he was very pleased with it all. You had best join us at lunch, and then you will see it for yourself."

After a hurried and frugal meal we were introduced with loving assiduity upon the part of the manager to the contents of his engine-house, and to the miscellaneous scrapheap of disused implements with which the grass was littered. On one side was a huge dismantled Arrol hydraulic shovel, with which the first excavations had been rapidly made. Beside it was a great engine which worked a continuous steel rope on which the skips were fastened which drew up the debris by successive stages from the bottom of the shaft. In the power-house were several Escher Wyss turbines of great horse-power running at one hundred and forty revolutions a minute and governing hydraulic accumulators which evolved a pressure of fourteen hundred pounds per square inch, passing in three-inch pipes down the shaft and operating four rock drills with hollow cutters of the Brandt type. Abutting upon the engine-house was the electric house supplying power for a very large lighting instalment, and next to that again was an extra turbine of two hundred horse-power, which drove a ten-foot fan forcing air down a twelve-inch pipe to the bottom of the workings. All these wonders were shown with many technical explanations by their proud operator, who was well on his way to boring me stiff, as I may in turn have done my reader. There came a welcome interruption, however, when I heard the roar of wheels and rejoiced to see my Leyland three-tonner come rolling and heaving over the grass, heaped up with tools and sections of tubing, and bearing my foreman, Peters, and a very grimy assistant in front. The two of them set to work at once to unload my stuff and to carry it in. Leaving them at their work, the manager, with Malone and myself, approached the shaft.

It was a wondrous place, on a very much larger scale than I had imagined. The spoil banks, which represented the thousands of tons removed, had been built up into a great horseshoe around it, which now made a considerable hill. In the concavity of this horseshoe, composed of chalk, clay, coal, and granite, there rose up a bristle of iron pillars and wheels from which the pumps and the lifts were operated. They connected with the brick power building which filled up the gap in the horseshoe. Beyond it lay the open mouth of the shaft, a huge yawning pit, some thirty or forty feet in diameter, lined and topped with brick and cement. As I craned my neck over the side and gazed down into the dreadful abyss, which I had been assured was eight miles deep, my brain reeled at the thought of what it represented. The sunlight struck the mouth of it diagonally, and I could only see some hundreds of yards of dirty white chalk, bricked here and there where the surface had seemed unstable. Even as I looked, however, I saw, far, far down in the darkness, a tiny speck of light, the smallest possible dot, but clear and steady against the inky background.

"What is that light?" I asked.

Malone bent over the parapet beside me.

"That's one of the cages coming up," said he. "Rather wonderful, is it not? That is a mile or more from us, and that little gleam is a powerful arc lamp. It travels quickly, and will be here in a few minutes."

Sure enough the pin-point of light came larger and larger, until it flooded the tube with its silvery radiance, and I had to turn away my eyes from its blinding glare. A moment later the iron cage clashed up to the landing stage, and four men crawled out of it and passed on to the entrance.

"Nearly all in," said Malone. "It is no joke to do a two-hour shift at that depth. Well, some of your stuff is ready to hand here. I suppose the best thing we can do is to go down. Then you will be able to judge the situation for yourself."

There was an annexe to the engine-house into which he led me. A number of baggy suits of the lightest tussore material were hanging from the wall. Following Malone's example I took off every stitch of my clothes, and put on one of these suits, together with a pair of rubber-soled slippers. Malone finished before I did and left the dressing-room. A moment later I heard a noise like ten dog-fights rolled into one, and rushing out I found my friend rolling on the ground with his arms round the workman who was helping to stack my artesian tubing. He was endeavouring to tear something from him to which the other was most desperately clinging. But Malone was too strong for him, tore the object out of his grasp, and danced upon it until it was shattered to pieces. Only then did I recognize that it was a photographic camera. My grimy-faced artisan rose ruefully from the floor.

"Confound you, Ted Malone!" said he. "That was a new ten-guinea machine."

"Can't help it, Roy. I saw you take the snap, and there was only one thing to do."

"How the devil did you get mixed up with my outfit?" I asked, with righteous indignation.

The rascal winked and grinned. "There are ways and means," said he. "But don't blame your foreman. He thought it was just a rag. I swapped clothes with his assistant, and in I came."

"And out you go," said Malone. "No use arguing, Roy. If Challenger were here he would set the dogs on you. I've been in a hole myself so I won't be hard, but I am watchdog here, and I can bite as well as bark. Come on! Out you march!"

So our enterprising visitor was marched by two grinning workmen out of the compound. So now the public will at last understand the genesis of that wonderful four-column article headed "Mad Dream of a Scientist" with the subtitle "A Bee-line to Australia," which appeared in *The Adviser* some days later and brought Challenger to the verge of apoplexy, and the editor of *The Adviser* to the most disagreeable and dangerous interview of his lifetime. The article was a highly coloured and exaggerated account of the adventure of Roy Perkins, "our experienced war correspondent," and it contained such purple passages as "this hirsute bully of Enmore Gardens," "a compound guarded by barbed wire, plug-uglies, and bloodhounds," and finally, "I was dragged from the edge of the Anglo-Australian tunnel by two ruffians, the more savage being a jack-of-all trades whom I had previously known by sight as a hanger-on of the journalistic profession, while the other, a sinister figure in a strange tropical garb, was posing as an Artesian engineer, though his appearance was more reminiscent of Whitechapel." Having ticked us off in this way, the rascal had an elaborate description of rails at the pit mouth, and of a zigzag excavation by which funicular trains were to burrow into the earth.

The only practical inconvenience arising from the article was that it notably increased that line of loafers who sat upon the South Downs waiting for something to happen. The day came when it did happen and when they wished themselves elsewhere.

My foreman with his faked assistant had littered the place with all my apparatus, my bellbox, my crowsfoot, the V-drills, the rods, and the weight, but Malone insisted that we disregard all that and descend ourselves to the lowest level. To this end we entered the cage, which was of latticed steel, and in the company of the chief engineer we shot down into the bowels of the earth. There were a series of automatic lifts, each with its own operating station hollowed out in the side of the excavation. They operated with great speed, and the experience was more like a vertical railway journey than the deliberate fall which we associate with the British lift.

Since the cage was latticed and brightly illuminated, we had a clear view of the strata which we passed. I was conscious of each of them as we flashed past. There were the sallow lower chalk, the coffee-coloured Hastings beds, the lighter Ashburnham beds, the dark carboniferous clays, and then, gleaming in the electric light, band after band of jet-black, sparkling coal alternating with the rings of clay. Here and there brickwork had been inserted, but as a rule the shaft was self-supported, and one could but marvel at the immense labour and mechanical skill which it represented. Beneath the coal-beds I was conscious of jumbled strata of a concrete-like appearance, and then we shot down into the primitive granite, where the quartz crystals gleamed and twinkled as if the dark walls were sown with the dust of diamonds. Down we went and ever down—lower now than ever mortals had ever before penetrated. The archaic rocks varied wonderfully in colour, and I can never forget one broad belt of rose-coloured feldspar, which shone with an unearthly beauty before our powerful lamps. Stage after stage, and lift after lift, the air getting ever closer and hotter until even the light tussore garments were intolerable and the sweat was pouring down into those rubber-soled slippers. At last, just as I was thinking that I could stand it no more, the last lift came to a stand and we stepped out upon a circular platform which had been cut in the rock. I noticed that Malone gave a curiously suspicious glance round at the walls as he did so. If I did not know him to be amongst the bravest of men, I should say that he was exceedingly nervous.

"Funny-looking stuff," said the chief engineer, passing his hand over the nearest section of rock. He held it to the light and showed that it was glistening with a curious slimy scum. "There have been shiverings and tremblings down here. I don't know what we are dealing with. The Professor seems pleased with it, but it's all new to me."

"I am bound to say I've seen that wall fairly shake itself," said Malone. "Last time I was down here we fixed those two cross-beams for your drill, and when we cut into it for the supports it winced at every stroke. The old man's theory seemed absurd in solid old London town, but down here, eight miles under the surface, I am not so sure about it."

"If you saw what was under that tarpaulin you would be even less sure," said the engineer. "All this lower rock cut like cheese, and when we were through it we came on a new formation like nothing on earth. 'Cover it up! Don't touch it!' said the Professor. So we tarpaulined it according to his instructions, and there it lies."

"Could we not have a look?"

A frightened expression came over the engineer's lugubrious countenance.

"It's no joke disobeying the Professor," said he. "He is so damn cunning, too, that you never know what check he has set on you. However, we'll have a peep and chance it."

He turned down our reflector lamp so that the light gleamed upon the black tarpaulin. Then he stooped and, seizing a rope which connected up with the corner of the covering, he disclosed half-a-dozen square yards of the surface beneath it.

It was a most extraordinary and terrifying sight. The floor consisted of some greyish material, glazed and shiny, which rose and fell in slow palpitation. The throbs were not direct, but gave the impression of a gentle ripple or rhythm, which ran across the surface. This surface itself was not entirely homogeneous, but beneath it, seen as through ground glass, there were dim whitish patches or vacuoles, which varied constantly in shape and size. We stood all three gazing spell-bound at this extraordinary sight.

"Does look rather like a skinned animal," said Malone, in an awed whisper. "The old man may not be so far out with his blessed echinus."

"Good Lord!" I cried. "And am I to plunge a harpoon into that beast!"

"That's your privilege, my son," said Malone, "and, sad to relate, unless I give it a miss-in-baulk, I shall have to be at your side when you do it."

"Well, I won't," said the head engineer, with decision.

"I was never clearer on anything than I am on that. If the old man insists, then I resign my portfolio. Good Lord, look at that!"

The grey surface gave a sudden heave upwards, welling towards us as a wave does when you look down from the bulwarks. Then it subsided and the dim beatings and throbbings continued as before. Barforth lowered the rope and replaced the tarpaulin.

"Seemed almost as if it knew we were here," said he.

"Why should it swell up towards us like that? I expect the light had some sort of effect upon it."

"What am I expected to do now?" I asked. Mr. Barforth pointed to two beams which lay across the pit just under the stopping place of the lift. There was an interval of about nine inches between them.

"That was the old man's idea," said he. "I think I could have fixed it better, but you might as well try to argue with a mad buffalo. It is easier and safer just to do whatever he says. His idea is that you should use your six-inch bore and fasten it in some way between these supports."

"Well, I don't think there would be much difficulty about that," I answered. "I'll take the job over as from to-day."

It was, as one might imagine, the strangest experience of my very varied life which has included well-sinking in every continent upon earth. As Professor Challenger was so insistent that the operation should be started from a distance, and as I began to see a good deal of sense in his contention, I had to plan some method of electric control, which was easy enough as the pit was wired from top to bottom. With infinite care my foreman, Peters, and I brought down our lengths of tubing and stacked them on the rocky ledge. Then we raised the stage of the lowest lift so as to give ourselves room. As we proposed to use the percussion system, for it would not do to trust entirely to gravity, we hung our hundred-pound weight over a pulley beneath the lift, and ran our tubes down beneath it with a V-shaped terminal. Finally, the rope which held the weight was secured to the side of the shaft in such a way that an electrical discharge would release it. It was delicate and difficult work done in a more than tropical heat, and with the ever-present feeling that a slip of a foot or the dropping of a tool upon the tarpaulin beneath us might bring about some inconceivable catastrophe. We were awed, too, by our surroundings. Again and again I have seen a strange quiver and shiver pass down the walls, and have even felt a dull throb against my hands as I touched them. Neither Peters nor I were very sorry when we signalled for the last time that we were ready for the surface, and were able to report to Mr. Barforth that Professor Challenger could make his experiment as soon as he chose.

And it was not long that we had to wait. Only three days after my date of completion my notice arrived.

It was an ordinary invitation card such as one uses for "at homes," and it ran thus:

>PROFESSOR G. E. CHALLENGER,
>
>F.R.S. MD., D.Sc., etc.
>
>>(late President Zoological Institute and holder of so many honorary degrees and appointments that they overtax the capacity of this card)

>   requests the attendance of
>   MR. JONES (no lady)
>   at 11:30 a.m. of Tuesday, June 21st, to witness a
>   remarkable triumph of mind over matter
>   at
>   HENGIST DOWN, SUSSEX.
>   Special train Victoria 10:05. Passengers pay their
>   own fares. Lunch after the experiment or not—
>   according to circumstances. Station, Storrington.
>   R.S.V.P. (and at once with name in block letters),
>   14 (Bis), Enmore Gardens, S.W.

I found that Malone had just received a similar missive over which he was chuckling. "It is mere swank sending it to us," said he. "We have to be there whatever happens, as the hangman said to the murderer. But I tell you this has set all London buzzing. The old man is where he likes to be, with a pin-point limelight right on his hairy old head."

And so at last the great day came. Personally I thought it well to go down the night before so as to be sure that everything was in order. Our borer was fixed in position, the weight was adjusted, the electric contacts could be easily switched on, and I was satisfied that my own part in this strange experiment would be carried out without a hitch. The electric controls were operated at a point some five hundred yards from the mouth of the shaft, to minimize any personal danger. When on the fateful morning, an ideal English summer day, I came to the surface with my mind assured, I climbed half-way up the slope of the Down in order to have a general view of the proceedings.

All the world seemed to be coming to Hengist Down. As far as we could see the roads were dotted with people. Motor-cars came bumping and swaying down the lanes, and discharged their passengers at the gate of the compound. This was in most cases the end of their progress. A powerful band of janitors waited at the entrance, and no promises or bribes, but only the production of the coveted buff tickets, could get them any farther. They dispersed therefore and joined the vast crowd which was already assembling on the side of the hill and covering the ridge with a dense mass of spectators. The place was like Epsom Downs on the Derby Day. Inside the compound certain areas had been wired-off, and the various privileged people were conducted to the particular pen to which they had been allotted. There was one for peers, one for members of the House of Commons, and one for the heads of learned societies and the men of fame in the scientific world, including Le Pellier of the Sorbonne and Dr. Driesinger of the Berlin Academy. A special reserved enclosure with sandbags and a corrugated iron roof was set aside for three members of the Royal Family.

At a quarter past eleven a succession of chars-a-bancs brought up specially-invited guests from the station and I went down into the compound to assist at the reception. Professor Challenger stood by the select enclosure, resplendent in frock-coat, white waistcoat, and burnished top-hat, his expression a blend of overpowering and almost offensive benevolence, mixed with most portentous self-importance.

"Clearly a typical victim of the Jehovah complex," as one of his critics described him. He assisted in conducting and occasionally in propelling his guests into their proper places, and then, having gathered the elite of the company around him, he took his station upon the top of a convenient hillock and looked around him with the air of the chairman who expects some welcoming applause. As none was forthcoming, he plunged at once into his subject, his voice booming to the farthest extremities of the enclosure.

"Gentlemen," he roared, "upon this occasion I have no need to include the ladies. If I have not invited them to be present with us this morning it is not, I can assure you, for want of appreciation, for I may say"—with elephantine humour and mock modesty—"that the relations between us upon both sides have always been excellent, and indeed intimate. The real reason is that some small element of danger is involved in our experiment, though it is not sufficient to justify the discomposure which I see upon many of your faces. It will interest the members of the Press to know that I have reserved very special seats for them upon the spoil banks which immediately overlook the scene of the operation. They have shown an interest which is sometimes indistinguishable from impertinence in my affairs, so that on this occasion at least they cannot complain that I have been remiss in studying their convenience. If nothing happens, which is always possible, I have at least done my best for them. If, on the other hand, something does happen, they will be in an excellent position to experience and record it, should they ultimately feel equal to the task.

"It is, as you will readily understand, impossible for a man of science to explain to what I may describe, without undue disrespect, as the common herd, the various reasons for his conclusions or his actions. I hear some unmannerly interruptions, and I will ask the gentleman with the horn spectacles to cease waving his umbrella. (A voice: 'Your description of your guests, sir, is most offensive.') Possibly it is my phrase, 'the common herd,' which has ruffled the gentleman. Let us say, then, that my listeners are a most uncommon herd. We will not quibble over phrases. I was about to say, before I was interrupted by this unseemly remark, that the whole matter is very fully and lucidly discussed in my forthcoming volume upon the earth, which I may describe with all due modesty as one of the epoch-making books of the world's history. (General interruption and cries of 'Get down to the facts!' 'What are we here for?' 'Is this a practical joke?') I was about to make the matter clear, and if I have any further interruption I shall be compelled to take means to preserve decency and order, the lack of which is so painfully obvious. The position is, then, that I have sunk a shaft through the crust of the earth and that I am about to try the effect of a vigorous stimulation of its sensory cortex, a delicate operation which will be carried out by my subordinates, Mr. Peerless Jones, a self-styled expert in Artesian borings, and Mr. Edward Malone, who represents myself upon this occasion. The exposed and sensitive substance will be pricked, and how it will react is a matter for conjecture. If you will now kindly take your seats these two gentlemen will descend into the pit and make the final adjustments. I will then press the electric button upon this table and the experiment will be complete."

An audience after one of Challenger's harangues usually felt as if, like the earth, its protective epidermis had been pierced and its nerves laid bare. This assembly was no exception, and there was a dull murmur of criticism and resentment as they returned to their places.

Challenger sat alone on the top of the mound, a small table beside him, his black mane and beard vibrating with excitement, a most portentous figure. Neither Malone nor I could admire the scene, however, for we hurried off upon our extraordinary errand. Twenty minutes later we were at the bottom of the shaft, and had pulled the tarpaulin from the exposed surface.

It was an amazing sight which lay before us. By some strange cosmic telepathy the old planet seemed to know that an unheard-of liberty was about to be attempted. The exposed surface was like a boiling pot. Great grey bubbles rose and burst with a crackling report. The air-spaces and vacuoles below the skin separated and coalesced in an agitated activity. The transverse ripples were stronger and faster in their rhythm than before. A dark purple fluid appeared to pulse in the tortuous anastomoses of channels which lay under the surface. The throb of life was in it all. A heavy smell made the air hardly fit for human lungs.

My gaze was fixed upon this strange spectacle when Malone at my elbow gave a sudden gasp of alarm. "My God, Jones!" he cried. "Look there!"

I gave one glance, and the next instant I released the electric connection and I sprang into the lift. "Come on!" I cried. "It may be a race for life!"

What we had seen was indeed alarming. The whole lower shaft, it would seem, had shared in the increased activity which we had observed below, and the walls were throbbing and pulsing in sympathy. This movement had reacted upon the holes in which the beams rested, and it was clear that a very little further retraction—a matter of inches—the beams would fall. If they did so then the sharp end of my rod would, of course, penetrate the earth quite independently of the electric release. Before that happened it was vital that Malone and I should be out of the shaft. To be eight miles down in the earth with the chance any instant of some extraordinary convulsion taking place was a terrible prospect. We fled wildly for the surface.

Shall either of us ever forget that nightmare journey? The lifts whizzed and buzzed and yet the minutes seemed to be hours. As we reached each stage we sprang out, jumped into the next lift, touched the release and flew onwards. Through the steel latticed roof we could see far away the little circle of light which marked the mouth of the shaft. Now it grew wider and wider, until it came full circle and our glad eyes rested upon the brickwork of the opening. Up we shot, and up—and then at last in a glad moment of joy and thankfulness we sprang out of our prison and had our feet upon the green sward once more. But it was touch and go. We had not gone thirty paces from the shaft when far down in the depths my iron dart shot into the nerve ganglion of old Mother Earth and the great moment had arrived.

What was it happened? Neither Malone nor I was in a position to say, for both of us were swept off our feet as by a cyclone and swirled along the grass, revolving round and round like two curling stones upon an ice rink. At the same time our ears were assailed by the most horrible yell that ever yet was heard. Who is there of all the hundreds who have attempted it who has ever yet described adequately that terrible cry? It was a howl in which pain, anger, menace, and the outraged majesty of Nature all blended into one hideous shriek. For a full minute it lasted, a thousand sirens in one, paralysing all the great multitude with its fierce insistence, and floating away through the still summer air until it went echoing along the whole South Coast and even reached our French neighbours across the Channel. No sound in history has ever equalled the cry of the injured Earth.

Dazed and deafened, Malone and I were aware of the shock and of the sound, but it is from the narrative of others that we learned the other details of that extraordinary scene.

The first emergence from the bowels of the earth consisted of the lift cages. The other machinery being against the walls escaped the blast, but the solid floors of the cages took the full force of the upward current. When several separate pellets are placed in a blow-pipe they still shoot forth in their order and separately from each other. So the fourteen lift cages appeared one after the other in the air, each soaring after the other, and describing a glorious parabola which landed one of them in the sea near Worthing pier, and a second one in a field not far from Chichester. Spectators have averred that of all the strange sights that they had ever seen nothing could exceed that of the fourteen lift cages sailing serenely through the blue heavens.

Then came the geyser. It was an enormous spout of vile treacly substance of the consistence of tar, which shot up into the air to a height which has been computed at two thousand feet. An inquisitive aeroplane, which had been hovering over the scene, was picked off as by an Archie and made a forced landing, man and machine buried in filth. This horrible stuff, which had a most penetrating and nauseous odour, may have represented the life blood of the planet, or it may be, as Professor Driesinger and the Berlin School maintain, that it is a protective secretion, analogous to that of the skunk, which Nature has provided in order to defend Mother Earth from intrusive Challengers. If that were so the prime offender, seated on his throne upon the hillock, escaped untarnished, while the unfortunate Press were so soaked and saturated, being in the direct line of fire, that none of them was capable of entering decent society for many weeks.

This gush of putridity was blown southwards by the breeze, and descended upon the unhappy crowd who had waited so long and so patiently upon the crest of the Downs to see what would happen. There were no casualties. No home was left desolate, but many were made odoriferous, and still carry within their walls some souvenir of that great occasion.

And then came the closing of the pit. As Nature slowly closes a wound from below upwards, so does the Earth with extreme rapidity mend any rent which is made in its vital substance. There was a prolonged high-pitched crash as the sides of the shaft came together, the sound, reverberating from the depths and then rising higher and higher until with a deafening bang the brick circle at the orifice flattened out and clashed together, while a tremor like a small earthquake shook down the spoil banks and piled a pyramid fifty feet high of debris and broken iron over the spot where the hole had been. Professor Challenger's experiment was not only finished, it was buried from human sight for ever. If it were not for the obelisk which has now been erected by the Royal Society it is doubtful if our descendants would ever know the exact site of that remarkable occurrence.

And then came the grand finale. For a long period after these successive phenomena there was a hush and a tense stillness as folk reassembled their wits and tried to realize exactly what had occurred and how it had come about. And then suddenly the mighty achievement, the huge sweep of the conception, the genius and wonder of the execution, broke upon their minds. With one impulse they turned upon Challenger. From every part of the field there came the cries of admiration, and from his hillock he could look down upon the lake of upturned faces broken only by the rise and fall of the waving handkerchiefs. As I look back I see him best as I saw him then. He rose from his chair, his eyes half closed, a smile of conscious merit upon his face, his left hand upon his hip, his right buried in the breast of his frock-coat. Surely that picture will be fixed for ever, for I heard the cameras clicking round me like crickets in a field.

The June sun shone golden upon him as he turned gravely bowing to each quarter of the compass. Challenger the super scientist, Challenger the arch-pioneer, Challenger the first man of all men whom Mother Earth had been compelled to recognize.

Only a word by way of epilogue. It is of course well known that the effect of the experiment was a world-wide one. It is true that nowhere did the injured planet emit such a howl as at the actual point of penetration, but she showed that she was indeed one entity by her conduct elsewhere. Through every vent and every volcano she voiced her indignation. Hecla bellowed until the Icelanders feared a cataclysm. Vesuvius blew its head off. Etna spewed up a quantity of lava, and a suit of half-a-million lira damages has been decided against Challenger in the Italian Courts for the destruction of vineyards. Even in Mexico and in the belt of Central America there were signs of intense Plutonic indignation, and the howls of Stromboli filled the whole Eastern Mediterranean. It has been the common ambition of mankind to set the whole world talking. To set the whole world screaming was the privilege of Challenger alone.

1928

List of Contributors

Joshua Glenn is a consulting semiotician and editor of the websites HiLobrow and Semiovox. The first to describe 1900–1935 as science fiction's "Radium Age," he is editor of the MIT Press's series of reissued proto-sf stories from that period. He is coauthor and co-editor of various books including, most recently, *Lost Objects* (2022).

Karel Čapek (1890–1938) was a Czech litterateur and anti-totalitarian absurdist who is best remembered today for his proto-science fiction efforts. These include the influential 1921 play *R.U.R.: Rossum's Universal Robots*, as well as the novels *The Absolute at Large* (1922), *Krakatit* (1924), and *War with the Newts* (1936).

Marie Corelli (Mary Mackay, 1855–1924) wrote popular bestsellers, many of which featured sf elements (interstellar travel, advanced technology), and all of which aimed to reconcile Christian teachings with Western esotericism. In addition to *The Young Diana* (1918), her Radium Age proto-sf writing includes the novel *The Secret Power* (1921).

Arthur Conan Doyle (1859–1930) was a Scottish physician and author who in 1887 introduced Sherlock Holmes, arguably the best-known fictional detective. Doyle's proto-sf series of Professor Challenger adventures include *The Lost World* (1912) and *The Poison Belt* (1913); both have been reissued in a single volume by The MIT Press.

Hugo Gernsback (1884–1967) was an American editor and magazine publisher. Among his publications—which gave E.E. "Doc" Smith, Fletcher Pratt, Edmond Hamilton, Jack Williamson, and others their start—was the pioneering sf magazine, *Amazing Stories*, as well as *Wonder Stories*. It was Gernsback who popularized the term "science fiction."

H. Rider Haggard (1856–1925) was an English author known for adventure fiction and science-fantasy romances set in exotic locations, predominantly Africa. Considered a pioneer of the Lost World subgenre, he is best remembered for *King Solomon's Mines* (1885), *She* (1886–1887), and these novels' various sequels, prequels, and crossovers.

Thea von Harbou (1888–1954) was a German writer famous for the screenplays she developed with director Fritz Lang. Lang's *Metropolis* (1927) and Harbou's 1925 novelization were written simultaneously; she also collaborated with Lang on the proto-sf films *The Girl in the Moon* (1929) and *The Testament of Dr. Mabuse* (1933).

Alfred Jarry (1873–1907) was a French absurdist author and philosopher best known for the play *Ubu roi* (1896) and its sequels, and for his development of the mock-science of 'pataphysics, which he'd adumbrate entertainingly via *Gestes et opinions du docteur Faustroll, pataphysicien* (1911). His most science-fictional work is *Le surmâle* (1901).

Jean de La Hire (Adolphe d'Espie, 1878–1956) was a prolific French author of popular fiction. His works of proto-sf interest include *La Roue Fulgurante* (1908) and *L'Europe future* (1916). He is best known for the proto-superhero Nyctalope sequence, seventeen stories in all—from *Le Mystère des XV* (1911) to *L'Énigme du Squelette* (1955).

George Bernard Shaw (1856–1950) was an Irish-born playwright, critic, and political activist who espoused utopian socialism and "creative evolution" (via eugenics). In addition to his proto-sf play *Back to Methuselah: A Metabiological Pentateuch* (1921), his works of sf interest include *Man and Superman* (1903) and *Buoyant Billions* (1948).

M. P. Shiel (1865–1947) was a Montserrat-born British writer whose proto-sf works include *The Purple Cloud* (1901), *The Lord of the Sea* (1901), *The Last Miracle* (1906), *The Isle of Lies* (1909), and *The Young Men Are Coming!* (1937). He has received attention as a writer of partial Black ancestry, and as a novelist of Caribbean origin.

Francis Stevens (Gertrude Barrows Bennett, 18
first American woman to publish widely in fantas
tion; she was an important influence on A. Merritt
proto-sf novel *The Heads of Cerberus* (1919) and sev
ries were reissued by The MIT Press in a collection
Yaszek.

Publisher contact:
The MIT Press
Massachusetts Institute of Technology
77 Massachusetts Avenue, Cambridge, MA 02139
mitpress.mit.edu

EU Authorised Representative:
Easy Access System Europe, Mustamäe tee 50,
10621 Tallinn, Estonia
gpsr.requests@easproject.com

Printed by Integrated Books International,
United States of America